Presented to:

From:

Date:

6

DUCK COMMANDER

Happy, Happy, Happy Stories for Kids

FUN AND FAITH-FILLED STORIES

Korie ROBERTSON & Chrys HOWARD

Illustrated by Holli Conger

Tommy NELSON

A Division of Thomas Nelson Publishers

DUCK COMMANDER

Happy, Happy, Happy Stories for Kids

FUN AND FAITH-FILLED STORIES

A Division of Thomas Nelson Publishers

Korie ROBERTSON & Chrys HOWARD

Illustrated by Holli Conger

Duck Commander Happy, Happy, Happy Stories for Kids

© 2017 Korie Robertson and Chrys Howard

All rights reserved. No portion of this book may be reproduced, stored in a retrieval system, or transmitted in any form or by any means—electronic, mechanical, photocopy, recording, scanning, or other—except for brief quotations in critical reviews or articles, without the prior written permission of the publisher.

Published in Nashville, Tennessee, by Tommy Nelson. Tommy Nelson is an imprint of Thomas Nelson. Thomas Nelson is a registered trademark of HarperCollins Christian Publishing, Inc.

The Duck Commander logo is used with permission.

Published in association with WME Entertainment, c/o Mel Berger and Margaret Riley King, 1325 Avenue of the Americas, New York, New York 10019.

Tommy Nelson titles may be purchased in bulk for educational, business, fund-raising, or sales promotional use. For information, please e-mail SpecialMarkets@ThomasNelson.com.

Unless otherwise noted, Scripture quotations are taken from the Holy Bible, New International Version®, NIV®. Copyright © 1973, 1978, 1984, 2011 by Biblica, Inc.® Used by permission of Zondervan. All rights reserved worldwide. www.zondervan.com. The "NIV" and "New International Version" are trademarks registered in the United States Patent and Trademark Office by Biblica, Inc.®

Scripture quotations marked ICB are from the International Children's Bible®. Copyright © 1986, 1988, 1999 by Thomas Nelson. Used by permission. All rights reserved.

Any Internet addresses, phone numbers, or company or product information printed in this book are offered as a resource and are not intended in any way to be or to imply an endorsement by Thomas Nelson, nor does Thomas Nelson vouch for the existence, content, or services of these sites, phone numbers, companies, or products beyond the life of this book.

ISBN 978-0-7180-8627-5
Library of Congress Cataloging-in-Publication Data is on file.

Printed in the United States of America
17 18 19 20 21 LSC 10 9 8 7 6 5 4 3 2 1
Mfr: LSC / Crawfordsville, IN / January 2017 / PO #9428689

This book is dedicated to the children in our family,
who continually teach us that life is an adventure worth
living, that love is always the right answer,
and that God truly can do more than we ask or imagine.

Contents

Introduction. x

1 The Birthday Party. 2

2 Farmhouse Fun 14

3 Survivor Day 26

4 The Treehouse. 48

5 The Easter Surprise 62

6 The Ski Trip 76

7 Lickety-Split. 96

8 The New Kid 110

9   Music Lessons 122

10   The Prank 134

11   Leap of Faith 146

12   Open and Honest 160

13   New Food 174

14   Little 192

    A Final Word 206

Introduction

To our readers . . .

We are happy, happy, happy that we were asked to write another book for children of all ages. *Duck Commander Happy, Happy, Happy Stories for Kids* is full of stories of the real-life adventures our family has experienced. From ski trips to chasing roosters, the Robertson clan loves to get together—and sometimes that leads to a little craziness. Our prayer is that these stories will entertain as well as inspire you. We know that Jesus taught using parables, which is another word for stories, and through those stories, many people have learned about God's love for them. We hope the same will be said about our stories.

It's been fun remembering events that have happened in our lives and writing about them. Then the special magic happens when

an artist draws and paints pictures to bring the stories to life! We love how colorful and fun the pages of this book are and want to thank the illustrator for her hard work.

We also want to thank you for wanting to read things that will bring you closer to God. Each chapter has a section called Duck Commander in Action. Those are your action steps to put into practice the biblical application of the story. Thank you in advance for doing what it takes to be more Christlike in all you do.

We hope you enjoy reading this book as much as we enjoyed writing it. Keep your eyes open and ears alert to God's calling in your life, and remember to tell your own stories around the dinner table or before bed at night.

No one's story is as good as your own!

Hugs and Blessings,
Korie and Chrys

Tell it to your children,
and let your children tell it
to their children,
and their children
to the next generation.

Joel 1:3

CHAPTER 1

The Birthday Party

Follow God's example, therefore,
as dearly loved children.
Ephesians 5:1

"Spending the night with cousins is the funnest thing to do!" Will yelled as he ran to his bedroom to get his backpack.

He looked carefully around the room, not wanting to forget anything important.

A football is super important, he thought to himself. The cousins might want to play a game in the dark, so he stuffed his football in the bag first.

Then Will looked under his bed and found his favorite blanket.

Mamaw Kay had made the blanket. It was soft and fuzzy with footballs all over it. He would definitely need his blanket. Not like a little-kid-attached-to-his-blankie kind of need. It was just really warm to sleep under.

Next Will opened his desk drawer and found his cards. At seven years old, Will was a master at Go Fish, and he knew his cousins liked to play too.

"What else? What else?" Will's eyes darted around his room and finally landed on a box filled with Legos. "Yes!" he said. "These have to go with me!"

Will's backpack was stuffed and ready to go when Aunt Ashley arrived to pick him up.

"Will! We're ready to go!"

Will was so excited he nearly ran out of the house without hugging his mom.

"Will Robertson!" Korie said, pretending to be angry, "You'd better come hug me good night."

"Love ya, Mom. See ya in the morning!" Will said as he quickly hugged Korie and ran out the front door.

Two of his cousins, Maddox and Asa, were already strapped in their seatbelts and waving for Will to jump in the van. Maddox is half a year younger than Will, and Asa is half a year older than Will. Will is *right* in the middle, and when the three of them together, "It's a . . . party," as Aunt Ashley, Maddox's mom, says.

And this day actually *was* a party. It was Maddox's birthday! Maddox didn't want a big party. He just wanted his cousins to spend the night and, of course, for them to go to their favorite places.

The first stop was Chik-fil-A. Will jumped out of the van first, followed by Maddox and Asa, and off they went.

"Chicken sandwich with cheese, no pickles!"

"Nuggets!"

"Chicken strips!"

"Coke!"

"Waffle fries!"

Everyone yelled their orders at one time.

Aunt Ashley put her hands over her ears. "One at a time, please!"

All three boys were quiet for a few minutes as they quickly gobbled down chicken and fries.

"Where are we going next?" Will asked, his mouth still full of chicken.

Maddox hadn't told them what they were doing for his birthday. He wanted it to be a surprise, but Will was too excited to wait.

"Maddox," his mom said, "do you want to tell them?"

Maddox looked at his cousins, their eyes wide. "Okay . . ." Maddox said. "We're going to ride go-carts!"

"YES! No way! I can't believe it! This will be SO COOL!"

The other customers in the restaurant nearly jumped out of their skins as the three boys screamed in excitement. Again, Aunt Ashley covered her ears and leaned forward. "We'd better get going before they kick us out."

Once they were back in the van, all the boys could think about was the go-carts and who would win.

"I'm sure I'll win," Asa said. "I'm the oldest and I've done it before. It was easy."

"You might be older, but I'm bigger," Will proudly announced. "I drove one at the last birthday party."

"It's *my* birthday," Maddox said. "I think I should win!"

"May the best driver win," Ashley said from the front seat. "Let's remember, this is for fun! Everyone just have a good time."

And they did. They got to ride three times, and guess what? Maddox won. Then Asa won. And then Will won!

Aunt Ashley took lots of pictures. With their helmets on, the boys looked like real race car drivers. One last pose with their arms around each other and off they went.

It was time to go to Maddox's house for sleepover fun.

Maddox's room was decorated with green tractors. He had a green tractor lamp and a bedspread and curtains with green tractors all over them.

But the boys didn't notice or care about what was on the bed or windows. They were too excited to take off their backpacks and start playing.

They played cards.

And Legos.

And football in the dark.

And watched a movie.

And ate popcorn.

And at midnight, they had cake and ice cream to celebrate Maddox's birthday.

It had been a long night of fun, but it was now time for bed.

Aunt Ashley sent everyone upstairs to brush their teeth and get their pajamas on.

Will grabbed his backpack and reached inside for his toothbrush and pajamas, but the backpack was empty.

He opened the front zipper hoping he had put them in there, but all he found was one sock from another sleepover.

Maybe I already took them out, Will thought to himself as he began searching Maddox's room while Asa and Maddox were busy getting ready for bed.

Nope. No extra toothbrushes or pajamas were laying around Maddox's room.

"Maddox," Will said. "I forgot my toothbrush and pajamas."

"It's okay," Maddox replied. "I think we have extras."

"Mo-om!" Maddox yelled down the stairs. "Will forgot his toothbrush and pajamas."

Aunt Ashley handed will a new toothbrush and some of Maddox's pajamas and ruffled his hair. "I guess when you were packing all the fun things, you forgot to pack the *important* things. Right, Will?"

"I guess you're right. The next time I spend the night, I'll put those things in first!"

WHAT DOES THE BIBLE SAY?

"Be dressed and ready for service and keep your lamps burning, like servants waiting for their master to return from a wedding banquet, so that when he comes and knocks they can immediately open the door for him."

LUKE 12:35-36

Let's Talk About It

What did Mamaw Kay make for Will

that he liked to sleep with? _____

Whose birthday party did Will go to? _____

What restaurant did the cousins stop to eat at? _____

_____

What time did they eat birthday cake and ice cream?

_____

Tell about a time when you weren't ready for an activity.

What happened? _____

_____

_____

_____

_____

DUCK Commander in ACTION

Being prepared means being ready. We have to be ready for lots of things. School, sports, church activities, and chores around the house are all things we have to be prepared or ready to do.

For school, you have to complete your homework and get your backpack ready. If you play sports, you need to practice and have your uniform clean and your equipment ready. To prepare for your chores around the house, you might need to start early in the day or get something out of the cabinet, like dog food or a broom.

Every activity we do requires some kind of preparation. Moms and dads like for kids to learn to be prepared without them having to remind you. As you get older, being prepared will get easier, but you will have to work on it.

INSTRUCTIONS

1
2
3

You can work on being prepared by using this method:

1. Stop: Sometimes you have to slow down so you can see what you need to do next. So slow it down. Or even stop! Then you can let your brain focus on what you need to do.

2. Look: Before you leave for an activity, train yourself to look around to be sure you have everything you need for the activity you will be doing.

3. Listen: Pay attention to any instructions given to you. Listen to your teacher, your coach, and your parents. That way you will know what is expected of you.

CHAPTER 2

Farmhouse Fun

But the Lord is faithful, and he will strengthen and protect you.
2 Thessalonians 3:3

Sadie ran as fast as her legs could carry her.

In the distance, she heard one of the girls scream and knew she needed to go help. All the girls had come to the farmhouse today while their moms cooked for a family hamburger supper.

The girls were all big enough to play outside alone, but Korie had told Sadie she was in charge. After all, she was the oldest. She was twelve, and the rest of the girls ranged from four to seven years old.

They had spent the morning playing one of their favorite games, hide-and-seek, in the big red barn, which was perfect and full of amazing hiding spots. The girls hid under the staircase, in the horses stalls, behind the old wagon wheel, and beneath the hay piled up in the back corner.

When they got bored with hiding, they wanted to fish in the pond, but the adults were all busy, and the lake was off limits if no adult was available.

"Maybe later," Korie told them as they sat in the kitchen eating peanut butter sandwiches for lunch. "Your dads will be here later. They can bait the hooks for you," she continued. "I'm sure we could fry up some catfish to go with our hamburgers tonight if one of you gets lucky and catches a big one."

It really was okay to save fishing for later because they hadn't had a chance to play with the animals yet.

Mamaw Kay loves animals, so she made sure the farmhouse had plenty. And a big fence to keep the animals from wandering off the property. Mamaw Kay called it a playpen for animals.

There were . . .
two horses,
three pigs,
two goats,
four sheep,
six chickens,
and one llama.

All the animals were very friendly and weren't scary to any of the kids—except one.

The rooster.

Mamaw Kay had told the girls, "That rooster has a temper like an old wet hen. Don't aggravate him."

As they finished their sandwiches, Mamaw Kay gave a little lesson on roosters. "A rooster's job is to protect the nest filled with eggs, so he's just being pro-tective, not mean. But it might seem like meanness!"

That made sense to Sadie. She had seen the rooster shoo away other animals or even people when they got close to the chickens' nests. *Maybe Mamaw Kay is right. Protecting someone is serious business.*

Soon lunch was over and the girls scattered to play with the animals.

Sadie went further out in the pasture than the little girls. She wanted to pet the horses. It was so peaceful out there. She looked up at the Louisiana spring sky and was so grateful for the warm sun on her arms and for how still and quiet everything was.

Then she heard the scream.

Sadie started running as fast as her legs would carry her to see who and where it had come from. The scream had startled her, and she suddenly felt guilty for wandering so far from the other girls. She could hear her mom's words: "Keep your eye on the little girls."

Sadie's heart was beating as fast as the wings on the butterfly she had tried to catch earlier that day. She now understood why the rooster

would flap his wings and squeal and squawk to protect those eggs. She felt like squealing herself!

I didn't realize I had gone this far into the pasture. Walking out here sure didn't seem to take as long as running back is taking! She picked up her pace.

Sadie ran past the sheep and goats, who were happily grazing in the grass.

She jumped over the fat little pigs as they waddled slowly to their trough.

She gave the llama a quick hello as she flew past him.

The chickens all scattered and clucked as she sprinted past them.

The only thing Sadie didn't see as she ran through the animal playpen was her cousins.

It was strange that none of them were in the fence with the animals. The last time she had looked back at them, some were chasing chickens and the others were feeding the llama.

Where are they? she thought. "Lily, Mia, Bella, Merritt!" she yelled as she rounded the corner of the last gate.

Out of breath, she finally stopped.

There stood four very calm little girls and one very scared black cat.

"Who screamed?" Sadie yelled. She didn't want to sound mad, but she was out of breath and worried, and her words seemed to pound out a little louder than she intended.

"It was the cat," Bella answered as she gently rubbed the cat's back in an effort to comfort her.

"What? A cat made all that noise?" Sadie demanded, still talking a little too loudly.

"Yeah," Lily said, motioning behind her. "Merritt found the cat trapped under the wheelbarrow. When we tried to help her out, she

got scared and screamed. We had never heard a cat scream like that, so we all got scared and screamed too. Sorry."

"She's good now," six-year-old Merritt chimed in, smiling with her no-front-teeth smile and nodding at the now-peaceful cat.

Sadie sat down on the ground and tried to catch her breath. Bella lowered the cat to the ground so she could get back to jumping and running after the farmhouse dog.

"We're sorry we scared you," sweet Priscilla said, giving Sadie a hug. "We were just trying to save the cat."

"It's okay," Sadie said, smiling at all the girls. "I was just trying to save *you*!"

Just then, the rooster let out a loud squawk and started chasing the cat. All five girls ran to rescue the cat from a very protective rooster.

WHAT DOES THE BIBLE SAY?

If you say, "The LORD is my refuge," and you make the Most High your dwelling, no harm will overtake you, no disaster will come near your tent. For he will command his angels concerning you to guard you in all your ways; they will lift you up in their hands, so that you will not strike your foot against a stone."

PSALM 91:9-12

Let's Talk About It

What game did the girl cousins love to play around the

barn? _____

What animal were they afraid of? _____

Why did Sadie get so far away from the rest of the girl?

Where was the cat trapped? _____

Can you tell about a time when you were scared?

_____

_____

_____

_____

_____

DUCK Commander in ACTION

Here's a simple way to learn about protection. Go outside and walk around your yard without your shoes on. Pay attention to the things your feet feel. You might find a sticker in the grass that pokes your foot or you might hit your toe on a tree root. You might feel the grass tickle your feet. Notice everything. Next, put on your shoes and go on the same walk. With your shoes on, you are protected from the roots, stickers, and tickly grass.

We do many things to protect our bodies from outside harm. Can you think of some more ways besides wearing shoes? What about a hat for your head when it's cold outside or sunscreen to protect your skin from the rays of the sun?

The great news is that God protects us so much better than shoes or sunscreen or fuzzy hats. God loves you so much that He wants to keep you from harm of any kind. You might face some scary situations, but God will always be with you. Isaiah 41:10 is another great verse to help us when we are scared. Write this verse on a piece of paper, and put it beside your bed to remind you that God is always with you.

So do not fear, for I am with you;
do not be dismayed, for I am your God.
I will strengthen you and help you;
I will uphold you with my righteous right hand.

CHAPTER 3

Survivor Day

Use whatever gift you have received to serve others, as faithful stewards of God's grace.

1 Peter 4:10

"Wake up!" counselor Margie said as she banged a big kitchen pan with a metal spoon. "Survivor day has begun!"

One of the best days at summer camp for Sadie was Survivor Day. It's a day when all the kids are challenged to work hard and do their best while participating in some really hard activities. Sadie had waited for this day all year long, and it was finally here. Today was the day!

As soon as Sadie heard Margie bang on the pan, her heart jumped up in her throat.

"Come on, Macy!" Sadie squealed as she shook Macy awake. "Get your shoes on. We've got to get down to the main area!"

Sadie's cousin Macy is two years younger than Sadie and loved Survivor Day too. But she didn't love waking up at four in the morning.

"Uggghhhh. Sadie, this is crazy! Why couldn't they wait until at least seven?" Macy moaned, feeling around for her for shoes with her eyes still closed.

"You can do it!" Sadie said excitedly. "But we have to hurry so we can get on a good team!"

"You know they won't let us be on the same team," Macy complained, despair in her voice. "They always split us up."

"Maybe not this year!" Sadie bounced back. "Just hurry!"

Soon they were running down the camp trail from the girls' village to the main area. The trail was only four feet wide, and trees of all kinds lined each side. Tall, stately pines, flowering dogwoods, and shiny sweetgums were scattered throughout the hundred acres that make up Camp Ch-Yo-Ca. Sadie loved to look at the trees when she wasn't busy racing to Survivor Day. Right now she was trying to keep from tripping over the roots as she scrambled past them.

Even though the trails were lined with lights, it wasn't like running in the daylight. Shadows could hide a root or a fallen branch from clear view. Sadie and all the campers had to keep a careful eye on their footsteps.

As they arrived in the main area, Sadie could see that she and Macy were some of the first to make it to the Box. The Box was a raised structure about four steps off the ground. It was where all the campers knew to come when the bell rang. A director or counselor was always at the Box with instructions for the next activity.

Macy bent over and held her aching side in order to catch her breath. "Sadie, go see what we're supposed to do," she said to her older cousin. "I'm just trying to breathe here."

Eager to hear what was next, Sadie went straight to the camp director.

"So Miss LinDee . . . what are we doing?" Sadie asked.

"You know I'm not going to tell you that," Miss LinDee said, laughing at Sadie's bravery. This was Sadie's third year at senior high camp so it would be her fifth Survivor Day, including her middle school camp years. Miss LinDee always kept the activities planned a secret until the day officially began.

"Come on, campers! Gather up around the Box!" Miss LinDee yelled into the megaphone she was holding. "We've got to get the games going!"

The sleepy campers crowded around the box, waiting for their instructions. Some were barely awake, and others were bouncing up and down like they had already had a strong cup of morning coffee.

"When I call out your name," Miss LinDee said, "go join your team. Remember, no switching teams. Once you're put on a team, that's who you'll learn to work with for the entire day, so do not ask me to switch teams."

Miss LinDee and the other directors had worked hard to get the teams just right, and they never let campers change teams. Macy and

Sadie rolled their eyes at each other as if to say, *Here we go again . . . on different teams*.

Miss LinDee called name after name as the ten teams were being formed. Sadie's name was called early because she was older than Macy and names were called according to grade level. Macy stood nervously awaiting her fate, saying a prayer that she and Sadie would *finally* get to be together.

"Macy Moore, team seven!" Miss LinDee called.

Did I hear that right? Macy thought. Sure enough, it was Sadie's team! In an instant, Macy forgot it was only 4:30 a.m. and jumped for joy. She ran to her new team, hugging her cousin and screaming with delight.

"We've got this!" Sadie said. "It's you and me and that new big guy from Texas, Rick, and AnnaBeth. Remember her? She's from Oklahoma

and plays volleyball. She's a great athlete and really smart. We're going to have an awesome day!"

"All right, everyone! Time for the first activity," Miss LinDee yelled from the Box. "Get your team together and make your team flag. You'll find the supplies by your team number in the gym. We'll see you back at the Box in thirty minutes with your team name on your flag."

The teams nearly trampled each other to get to the supplies in the gym, but soon all the teams were quiet as they worked on choosing a team name and making their flag.

"Hey, everyone," Sadie said. "Before camp I looked up some Greek words that might be good to use. I found out that the word *Andreas* can be used for both male and female names and means "warrior." Do y'all like that?"

Sadie and Macy's entire team liked the name, so some of the more artistic kids starting painting the flag. Then each team member signed his or her name to the flag, and they headed to the Box.

Sadie, being very competitive, looked over at her team as they walked to the Box. Their team had sixteen total players with a variety of abilities. Sadie could already tell that some of them would be more suited for the mental games and others the physical games. She and Macy would be good for all the physical games, and AnnaBeth was really smart and could help with the mental games, but there were two kids Sadie didn't know anything about.

"What about those two?" Sadie whispered to Macy. "Do you think they can swim or paddle a boat or run? Or should we save them for the mental challenges later?"

Macy and Sadie knew the rules for the challenge games—no player could sit out in back-to-back challenges. If campers were tired, they could get a little break—but not for very long. This rule also kept campers from not participating at all. The directors called it "forced fun." Sadie never could understand why anyone would have to be *forced* to participate! This was her favorite day of the whole summer!

"I don't know," Macy whispered back. "They sure don't look very strong or fast. But we can't tell if they're smart either."

"I know," Sadie said. "But maybe it's better to save them and go ahead and get some points early in the day."

"Sounds good," Macy said.

Miss LinDee quickly gave them instructions for the first activity, and two hundred campers started running once again. Some went to

the lake, some to the baseball field, some to the archery range, and some to the pool. If a helicopter had been flying above, they would have seen what looked like groups of ants working together to build an ant farm. Each team huddled together as they made their way to their first challenge.

Team Andreas was sent to the pool challenge first, which made Sadie very happy. She *loved* the pool challenge. She knew not all the team members would be strong swimmers, but she hoped that enough of them would be to win the challenge.

"Does anyone want to sit out?" Sadie asked her team, remembering that two could sit out but that those two would have to play the next game. "If nobody wants to sit out, we'll draw straws."

Sure enough, the two campers Sadie and Macy were worried about raised their hands.

"Okay, great," Sadie said. "We'll get you two in later. What are your names? I don't think we've met yet."

"I'm Renee."

"I'm Randall."

"Are y'all related?" Sadie asked.

"We're twins," they answered.

"Wow! That's fun. Great to meet both of you," Sadie responded. "We're going to have a great day."

But the two siblings looked like they weren't too sure about Sadie's last words. This was their first year at camp, and Survivor Day seemed a little too intense for them.

Sadie quickly organized the rest of the team into relay formation and waited for the whistle to blow. First one swimmer, then the next, then another—all touching the side of the pool as they finished their turn racing across it. It was a close race, but Team Andreas pulled off the victory and got their first points of the day!

But as the day continued, Team Andreas struggled. The mental challenge was a puzzle made up of carpet squares that required the campers to remember a pattern to get each player across the puzzle. Macy and Sadie sat out of that challenge and cheered from the side. AnnaBeth did great, but it wasn't quite enough. Another team finished a few seconds quicker, giving Andreas the points for second place. Still, they were proud of their team.

Off they went to the tug-of-war. The tug-of-war pit was a mud hole filled with water. It was slippery, and many times even the team with the biggest boys didn't win because someone slipped. Just because Team Andreas had Rick didn't mean they'd win.

"Rick," Sadie said, "you need to be the last one lined up on the rope. You're our anchor. We're counting on you to get us this win."

"I got this," Rick said. The team lined up with their hands tightly on the rope. Rick took the last position at the end of the rope, anchored his feet, and prepared for battle. Randall and Renee were put in the front, where Sadie hoped they wouldn't get too hurt. The whole team pulled and tugged until their hands hurt, but it was worth it when they pulled the other team across the big

PULL!

mud hole. Everybody laughed. They were covered in mud but hugged each other anyway over their victory.

"Great job!" Sadie said to her teammates. "We're tied for first place! All we have to do is win the boat race."

The boat race was the toughest challenge. It required all the campers except the designated captain to start on one side of the lake. The captain had to paddle the boat alone to pick up two or three campers and take them back to the other side. Once other campers were in the boat, they could help the captain paddle, but after they were dropped off, the captain had to paddle back for more campers by himself or herself. This would go on until all the campers were across the lake.

"Let's think of our strategy. Rick, you're the biggest guy on our team. I know you've done a lot today, but I think you should be the captain. Do you feel good about paddling the boat?" Sadie asked.

"Seriously, Sadie, I have never paddled a boat," Rick said.

Sadie's heart sunk. All day she had watched big Rick and thought he was going to be the one to save the day.

"I'll do it," Randall said quietly from the back of the group.

Sadie's heart sunk again as she looked at Randall. While Rick looked like an athlete, Randall looked like he hadn't even bowled on a Wii. It was like David and Goliath. Their chances of winning the day seemed to be slipping away like Randall's feet did in the mud hole during the tug-of-war. Now Randall was volunteering to paddle the entire team across the lake!

Sadie swallowed hard and repeated to herself, *It's not whether you win or lose; it how you play the game.* Her grandma used to tell her that, but for some reason, she still liked the winning part best.

Oh well, today's not that day, she thought.

"Great, Randall! Thanks for volunteering," Sadie said.

"Macy, you go in the first group. AnnaBeth, you in the second. Rick, in the third. And I'll go with the fourth group. That way we'll have someone strong in each group," Sadie declared.

Miss LinDee blew the whistle, and the race was on. To Sadie's surprise, Randall was holding his own. He was paddling smoothly and was in second place when he arrived to pick up the first group. Macy and two other campers put on their life jackets and jumped in the boat. Macy picked up the other paddle and started paddling.

"No," Randall said calmly. "Paddle backward for a minute."

Macy paddled backward and the boat quickly turned around and headed to the opposite side. Macy gave Sadie a thumbs up signal.

They were still neck and neck with the other team, fighting for a first place finish as Randall pulled in for group two. AnnaBeth grabbed the other paddle and, once again, Randall calmly told her to paddle backward. Soon they were on their way to the other shore. And this time, the other team struggled to back away from the shoreline, giving Team Andreas the lead.

Sadie smiled. *Someone should tell the other team to paddle backward, but it's not going to be me!*

Soon Randall was back for group three.

"Rick!" Sadie hollered. "Listen to Randall! He knows what he's doing. Group three, get ready!"

But Rick had already been watching the race and knew that Randall could paddle a boat. He had his life jacket on and was ready for his instructions. Paddling was not his thing. He sure was glad it was Randall's!

"Come on!" Sadie yelled across the lake. They were in the lead—but barely. The other team gained on them while Rick's group made its way across the lake. Rick was right: he couldn't paddle a boat! In fact, his strength seemed to work against him as he paddled first one way and then another trying to get in rhythm with Randall.

This looks so simple, Rick thought. *What is my problem?*

Sadie got her group ready as she saw Randall heading back to pick them up.

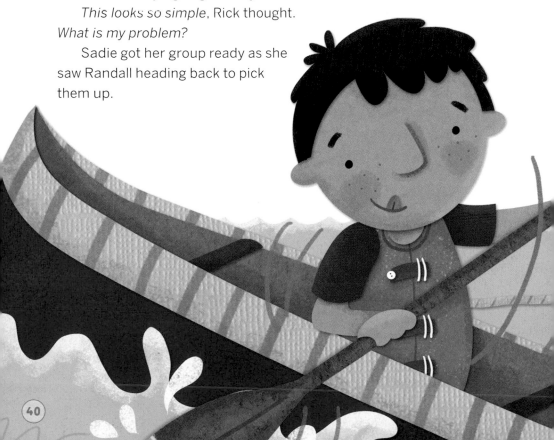

"This is it, Andreas!" Sadie yelled. "We can do this. We just have to get this last group across."

By now Randall was exhausted. He had paddled back and forth across the lake seven times, and his arms were beginning to feel like that Jello salad his grandma made at Thanksgiving. The only good news was the other team captains looked like they felt the same way. Sadie and her group jumped in the boat, and Sadie grabbed the extra paddle.

"Sadie," Randall said, "if you don't mind, can Renee have the other paddle."

It took Sadie a few seconds to realize she wasn't going to be saving the day, which she was used to doing. She loved sports and played most

of them—softball, basketball, tennis, and track—and she was almost always the strongest on the team. But today a twin brother-and-sister team were taking over.

"Sure . . ." Sadie said a little reluctantly as she handed the paddle to Renee.

Randall didn't say a word to Renee. She knew exactly what to do. She started paddling backward until the boat was turned around and perfectly lined up with the opposite shoreline. And then they started paddling together like a well-oiled machine. Their boat cut across the water like a warm knife through butter. Sadie looked to the right and left and saw that the other three teams weren't anywhere near them.

Then she looked at Randal and Renee, both smiling proudly as they worked together.

They reached the shore to high-fives and cheers from the rest of Team Andreas.

"We are truly a team of warriors!" Sadie said. "Every team of warriors has its stronger players. Today we learned that strength comes in many forms. Randall and Renee, you paddled us to victory! Where did you learn that?"

"We're on a rowing team in Mississippi. I'm glad we could help," Randall said. "That tug-of-war thing just wasn't for us! We're glad Rick is as strong as a bull."

The whole team laughed and hugged as they made their way to the Box for the medal ceremony. But inside, they knew that learning to work together and trust each other was the best reward of the day.

WHAT DOES THE BIBLE SAY?

For we are God's handiwork,
created in Christ Jesus to do good
works, which God prepared in
advance for us to do.

EPHESIANS 2:10

Let's Talk About It

What was Sadie's counselor's name? _____

How did she wake the campers up? _____

What did Sadie's team pull the other team over in the

tug-of-war competition? _____

What did Randall's arm feel like after paddling the boat?

_____

Name two talents or gifts you have. _____

_____

What are some ways you could use your talents to serve

God and help others? _____

_____

_____

_____

DUCK Commander in ACTION

God made each one of us with different gifts and talents. You might have a brother who can play an instrument or a sister who is good at drawing or a friend who is good at basketball. The important thing to remember is that God decided to give you the talents you have; you don't get to choose.

Have you ever watched a talent show? A talent show is a great way to see how God made everyone differently. Someone might sing. Someone else might do magic tricks. Others might play the piano. Those are different kinds of gifts.

Today would be a good day to organize a family talent show. Tell everyone in your family, including your mom and dad, that you want to have a talent show. Once you've decided on a time, you can start working on your talent. It will be fun to see what everyone decides to do.

Here are a few important things to remember about talents:

1. **God is in charge of giving out talents, not us.** It is our job to be thankful to God and then use our talents wisely. Be sure to thank God before your talent show for the talents you are about to see.

2. **Never get jealous of someone else's talent.** Remember God gave them that talent! Learn to celebrate others' gifts. While at the talent show, be sure to clap for each person, letting them know their hard work paid off.

3. **Using our talent requires work.** God didn't give us a talent so it could sit there unused. He gave us talents so we can show others what God did for us—and sometimes that takes work. If you are good at music or sports, you still have to practice.

4. **When others tell you that you have done a good job, thank them politely.** Being respectful about our talents lets others know we are thankful to God for them.

5. **Every talent requires training.**

6. **This one is important! Not all talents involve music or art or sports.** The Bible tells us that some people have the gift of encouraging others and or the gift of teaching and preaching. Your talent might include being a friend to others and helping others when they are discouraged. Don't worry—everyone has talents and gifts. If you haven't found yours yet, be patient and pay attention. You'll find them!

CHAPTER 4

The Tree House

Truly [God] is my rock and my salvation; he is my fortress. I will never be shaken.

Psalm 62:2

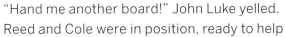

"Hand me another board!" John Luke yelled.

Reed and Cole were in position, ready to help John Luke get the boards he needed for the tree house. They had built the steps first, knowing they had to have a way to get each board up the tree. But the steps had been easy compared to the rest of the tree house.

John Luke was the main carpenter. After all, it was his house and his woods.

John Luke lived in the woods by Camp Ch-Yo-Ca. Camp Ch-Yo-Ca is a camp where kids go every summer and spend a week doing all kinds of fun activities.

Ch-Yo-Ca sounds like a Native American name, but it stands for Christian Youth Camp— Christian Youth Camp. Get it? John Luke's great-grandfather had built the camp many years earlier as a place for kids to go in the summer and learn about God.

At camp, kids can play different sports like softball, basketball, and volleyball. They can also go to the craft shed and paint rocks or make a pair of moccasins. Down one of the trails in the woods is a lake. Camp kids love to fish or go boating.

But one of the most important things at camp is the huge swimming pool. It has two diving boards and enough room for over a hundred kids! The pool is important because in Louisiana, the summers can get very hot. Jumping into a pool is the best way to cool off.

While they're at camp, all the campers live in cabins, but John Luke's family had a house a ways up the road from camp. When John Luke wanted to go to the camp to play, he would just walk down the road.

On his walk there, he would pass Miss Mary Lou's house. Sometimes he would stop and visit Miss Mary Lou. She lived in the first house on the right side of the camp road. She had a big dinner bell hanging outside her house. John Luke loved to ring the dinner bell. Many times, Miss Mary Lou would make cookies, and they would sit on the front porch and watch the cars go by.

After his visit, John Luke would walk past the softball field that is surrounded by wooden crosses. Then he would pass the sand volleyball court and the tennis court and the archery range. Then he would be at camp. It was a pretty long walk for a kid, but he didn't mind it at all. He loved camp.

During the summer months, camp would be full of kids doing every activity, but when camp was over, John Luke would be at camp all by himself, which he didn't mind at all. All by himself except for his daddy. His daddy worked at camp, so he was always there.

John Luke's dad's job was to make sure everything at camp worked properly. He was the one who mowed the grass and fixed the broken swings and put toilet paper in the bathrooms. His job was very important because the boys and girls who came to camp every summer needed a safe place to stay. John Luke's daddy made camp safe.

So when the campers weren't at camp, John Luke and his dad were there—making it safe.

And one more person was always there too: Mr. Dewie.

John Luke loved helping his dad around the camp, and he learned a lot from watching him work. And John Luke's dad learned a lot from watching Mr. Dewie.

Mr. Dewie was Miss Mary Lou's husband. It seemed to John Luke that Mr. Dewie didn't talk much, but he worked a lot.

Sometimes when John Luke would tell him something, Mr. Dewie would just say, "Whatever's right." John Luke wasn't sure what he meant, but he loved talking to Mr. Dewie anyway.

Mr. Dewie had a truck and a dog named Dude. Miss Mary Lou wanted to name the dog Snowflake, but Mr. Dewie said no—because he's a dude so his name is Dude. It seemed like that's all Mr. Dewie needed in life—a truck and a dog.

When Mr. Dewie got ready to go somewhere, he would just open the door of his truck and Dude would jump in. Then he would sit in Mr. Dewie's lap and look out the window as they rode to get the mail or take Miss Mary Lou to get groceries.

When Dude wasn't with Mr. Dewie, he would follow John Luke around the woods between Mr. Dewie's house and John Luke's house.

John Luke loved the woods. He spent hours exploring

and even made a map so he could remember where everything was. Sometimes he would find an animal bone or some other treasure to put in a cardboard box and save. His favorite treasure was the occasional snakeskin. He would nail the snakeskins to a board and display them in his room.

Dude loved to explore too. He would sniff at leaves and chase butterflies. John Luke loved Dude about as much as Mr. Dewie loved him.

Sometimes Mr. Dewie and John Luke's daddy had a building project at camp and would save the extra boards for John Luke to use for his projects.

So far, John Luke had built a rabbit cage and a bookcase for his room. Mr. Dewie had showed John Luke how to line up the boards and

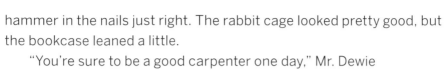

hammer in the nails just right. The rabbit cage looked pretty good, but the bookcase leaned a little.

"You're sure to be a good carpenter one day," Mr. Dewie encouraged, ruffling John Luke's hair. "Right now you're still learning."

And now John Luke and his cousins, Reed and Cole, were busy building a new tree house. It was a big project! Mr. Dewie and Dude were down at camp helping John Luke's daddy fix a broken washing machine. But John Luke and the boys were doing fine without them. "I can't wait to show Mr. Dewie how much better I've gotten," John Luke told his cousins as they continued to work.

When John Luke needed a new board, he would yell down to Reed, who was on the third step . . . and then Reed would yell to Cole, who was on the ground. Cole would choose a good board and hand it up to Reed who, would hand it to John Luke. Then the hammering would begin.

The system was working great, and the tree house was nearly finished. The boys were so excited to show Mr. Dewie, Willie, and of course, Dude.

"One more . . ." John Luke said, which let his cousins know he was almost finished.

"Here you go," Reed answered as he handed the last board to his cousin.

"Can I come up?" Cole asked from the ground. He had spent the whole day on the ground and was eager to climb something.

"Not yet," John Luke answered. "Remember, Dad said he or Mr. Dewie have to test it before we can play in it."

"But I'm ready now!" Cole said, kicking at the dirt. "You built it. It's gonna be fine."

"Nope," John Luke said. "We have to wait. They'll be here soon. Move over. I'm coming down."

John Luke climbed down the ladder and looked up at their masterpiece. "Wow!" he said. "I didn't think we could do it, but we did. It looks pretty cool!"

"Yeah," Reed added, "and wait until we get some chairs in there and maybe a TV."

John Luke laughed. "I don't think we'll get a TV, but it'll be a great place to read a book."

Reed wasn't very interested in reading a book in the tree house, but he was happy to have a new tree house to play in no matter what.

The boys heard the crunch of wheels on ground and looked up to see Mr. Dewie's truck coming down the driveway. Dude's head was peeping out the window. Behind the truck was John Luke's dad on the camp golf cart.

"Well, boys, you did it," Mr. Dewie said as he looked up in the tree, hand on hip. "It looks good, but will it hold an old man like me? Just because something looks good doesn't mean it is good."

The boys held their breath as Mr. Dewie took the first step . . .

then the second . . .

then the third . . .

until he stretched his legs up into the tree house.

Reed whispered to John Luke, "What are we gonna do if he comes crashing down?"

"I don't know," John Luke said. "Praying might be a good idea."

But John Luke knew he had done what Mr. Dewie had taught him. He had built the floor of the tree house first and made sure it was rock-solid before he did anything else. He had anchored the floorboards to the strongest branches so it was secure and stable.

All three boys had their eyes locked on the tree house door, waiting for Mr. Dewie to come out and tell them if the house passed inspection. They could hear him jumping up and down, and their eyes got bigger as they watched the house shake. But it didn't fall.

Then it happened.

Nothing but a thumb emerged from the door of the tree house—but it was a thumbs up sign.

The boys high-fived each other and yelled and screamed until the whole family came from the nearby houses to see what all the commotion was about.

The tree house was declared a success! John Luke hurried up the ladder and proudly waved down at his family.

"Come on, Reed and Cole! We can all fit!" John Luke said. "And bring Dude too. What good is a tree house without a tree house dog?"

WHAT DOES THE BIBLE SAY?

"Therefore everyone who hears these words of mine and puts them into practice is like a wise man who built his house on the rock."

MATTHEW 7:24

Let's Talk About It

What is the name of the camp John Luke lives beside?

_____

Which cousin stayed on the ground while the tree house

was built? _____

What did Reed want to put in the tree house? _____

_____

What was the name of the dog in the story? _____

_____

Share one memory verse you have learned.

_____

_____

_____

DUCK Commander in ACTION

Imagine that you've been told to build a house. You are given several big boards and several small, thin boards. What boards would you put on the bottom, or the floor, of the house? You'd put the bigger boards down first because they would be stronger. Right? Every building has to have a strong foundation. A foundation is what the house is built on. If the foundation is weak, the house might fall. But if the foundation is strong, the house could stand forever.

The Bible tells us that the Word of God is our foundation. That means if we read God's Word and do what it says, we'll be stronger people. Jesus wants us to be strong so we can fight the devil and his evil ways. One of the ways we know we can get stronger is by memorizing scriptures. Think about it like this: When you put on clothes, the clothes protect your body from the sun, the rain, and the cold. When you put Bible verses in your mind, they will help protect you when you might be afraid or tired or lonely.

Here are some important verses to get you started. To start, try to memorize one per week. You can choose your own verse if you want. Read each verse out loud. Then write it on a notecard and put it on your mirror in your bathroom or on the refrigerator so you can see multiple times a day. Try to say the verse you chose out loud three times a day. By the end of the week, you'll have it memorized and you'll be ready to memorize another!

Isaiah 43:5:
"Do not be afraid, for I am with you."

1 Corinthians 10:31:
So whether you eat or drink or whatever you do,
do it all for the glory of God.

Matthew 22:39:
"And the second is like it:
'Love your neighbor as yourself.'"

CHAPTER 5

The Easter Surprise

Share with God's people
who need help. Bring strangers
in need into your homes.

Romans 12:13 ICB

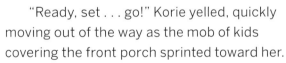

"Ready, set . . . go!" Korie yelled, quickly moving out of the way as the mob of kids covering the front porch sprinted toward her.

The "family and friends" Easter egg hunt had become a favorite day for Sadie. It was the one day when both sides of Sadie's big family could celebrate a holiday together. It's not that they didn't want to celebrate all the holidays together. There were just too many of them to get everyone in one place.

Since Easter is in the spring, when the weather is mild, the family could spread out in the yard and on the porches, giving them lots of room. So every Easter, the families would come together for lunch, Easter games, and an egg hunt.

This year, the big event was at Sadie's grandmother's house. Sadie and all the kids call her 2-Mama. Her house has a big front porch so all the adults can sit and watch as the kids scurry to collect eggs.

And 2-Mama has a big front yard with lots of hiding places. Eggs would be hidden be in the tall grass or tucked under the base of a tree or nestled down in an azalea bush, amid its bright pink flowers.

Earlier that day, the family had been at church together. Sadie loved being surrounded by her loved ones at church. She knew exactly where everyone would sit, and Easter Sunday was no different. There was Mamaw Jo, Aunt Jessi, Uncle Bill, and Aunt Carol over to her left. Uncle Randy and Aunt Joneal, with more big and little cousins, were directly behind her. Mamaw Kay and Papaw Phil were across the aisle but still close enough for Mamaw Kay to give Sadie a wink and a smile.

Uncle Jep, Aunt Jessica, and their kids filled up nearly an entire row right behind Mamaw Kay. Uncle Alan and Aunt Lisa were closer to the front. Uncle Alan used to be the preacher and would be leading a prayer today.

Aunt Missy and Uncle Jeremy were in their usual spots— singing on the worship team.

Sadie looked around. *Someone is missing. Where is Uncle Si?*

Then she spotted him. Uncle Si was leaning over giving a toddler a hug. Despite his scraggy beard and rough voice, kids love Uncle Si.

Sadie smiled as she took her place right between her mom and 2-Mama. Her dad, brothers, sisters, and more cousins filled up the same row she was sitting on.

Soon everyone was singing and praising God for sending His Son to earth. Sadie heard Uncle Si's booming voice over everyone else's and felt good that her whole family was together worshiping God.

After church, everyone made their way to 2-Mama's house. Cars lined her driveway, and kids poured out of the cars, carrying their empty Easter baskets.

Sadie parked behind Aunt Jessica and happily carried her newest cousin, baby Gus, to the house while Jessica unloaded the rest of the kids and their Easter baskets.

This is Gus's first Easter, Sadie thought. *Wow . . . how it that this is my eighteenth Easter? I'm hardly one of the kids anymore!*

Sadie gave Gus a quick kiss on the cheek and joined the rest of the family for a song and a prayer before lunch. She could smell the food and, of course, as part of their Easter tradition, spotted deviled eggs circling a plate. They were just waiting for her to grab one.

After the prayer, Sadie filled her plate with all the homemade goodies—ham, corn, potato casserole, green beans, and lots of desserts made by the different grandmas. Sadie's favorite was strawberry shortcake.

"Mom, I've already eaten two pieces!" Sadie told Korie. "And if there's any left, I'm taking it home!"

"You might need to hunt eggs today to burn off some calories!" Korie said, laughing as Sadie reached for another piece.

After lunch, Sadie stood on the front porch watching her parents, aunts, and uncles quickly hide nearly six hundred brightly colored eggs. *Six hundred eggs!* She thought about how funny it looked to see her duck-hunting, camo-wearing, truck-driving dad gently placing a pink egg in the perfect spot in the bend of a tree. Her mom looked pretty funny too in her fancy Easter dress and house slippers. Her mom couldn't move fast enough in her high heels.

I'm not going to be sad today—even though I know everything is about to change. In two months, Sadie would graduate from high school and move on to a more grown-up life. Today would be her last true kid-activity day.

Sadie walked back into the house to find the little cousins in the living room. Games and coloring books were keeping them busy until it was time to hunt eggs.

She sat down by her cousin River.

"River, what do you like about Easter?" Sadie asked.

"Candy!" River said.

"Good answer!" Sadie

high-fived her little cousin.

She reached over to pick up a small bean bag to toss at the Easter bunny game propped up near the wall.

"Try to make it in the middle hole," Priscilla told her. "That one is worth twenty-five points."

Sadie tossed the bean bag, and sure enough, it went right in the hole.

"Good job, Sadie!" Priscilla said, proud of her big cousin.

Sadie walked to the back porch to find another generation of family. The grandmas and great-grandmas were enjoying some time to visit.

"The lunch was delicious!" Sadie told all the ladies.

"Well, we're glad you liked it, honey," Mamaw Kay answered. "Did you try the strawberry shortcake?"

"Three times!" she said, and all the grandmas laughed.

"Everyone come to the front porch. It's time for the egg hunt!" Korie yelled to the entire houseful of people.

Everyone came running. The kids grabbed their baskets and lined up on the steps of the porch for instructions.

"Remember, some of the eggs have money in them. As long as you're still in school, you can hunt eggs," Korie said, looking right at Sadie. She knew Sadie was undecided about participating in the hunt today.

"One more thing. If you're one of our bigger hunters, leave the more obvious eggs for the little ones."

The kids started to get wiggly waiting for Korie to give them the signal that they could go.

Even though most of the eggs were in plain view, the egg hunters took the job of hunting very seriously. Most had already plotted their path and knew which direction they were going to run first.

"I'm going to the big bush by the flagpole," Lily told Rowdy.

"Okay, I'm going to the one by the mailbox," Rowdy said.

Sadie wanted to join the other kids, but she was almost grown. *Should I?* She stood on the porch with the older cousins, watching the little ones line up.

"Cole," Sadie said. "It's our last year. You wanna hunt?"

"I think I'm done hunting for Easter eggs," Cole replied.

"Okay . . ."

"Ready, set . . . go!" Korie yelled.

And they were off!

The front yard was soon covered with kids, running and squealing as they filled their baskets with eggs.

Sadie looked over to see a family who was visiting today. They were new to the area and looked like they didn't have much. Her mom and dad had met them at church and invited them over for the day. They had one little boy who was about three years old and a brand-new baby. Sadie suddenly realized how blessed she had been to have a family to share Easter egg hunts with.

"I'm going. It's my last chance!" Sadie told Cole as she grabbed an extra basket from the porch and joined the other kids.

The younger cousins loved having Sadie out there with them. They

laughed as their big cousin jumped up to rescue an egg from the tall branches of an oak tree and then carefully crawled under a rose bush, narrowly escaping the sticky thorns.

One by one, the eggs disappeared from the yard and filled the baskets.

Some of the kids sat down in the grass with their full baskets and began opening each egg to see what treat it held. But others were still looking under leaves and inside bushes in case there were more to be found.

Sadie sat next to the new little boy and found out his name was Jacob.

"Jacob, do you want to help me open my eggs?" she asked.

Jacob was shy at first, but after the first egg revealed a candy treat, he joined in the fun.

Jacob eagerly helped Sadie open all her Easter eggs. Her grand total was five pieces of gum, seven jelly beans, nine partially melted chocolate balls, and thirty-four dollars! That was the most money she had ever found at an Easter egg hunt.

She went inside the house and found a small sack in the kitchen. She wrote Jacob's name on the sack and put all the candy inside it. Then she found her wallet, which she knew had twenty dollars in it. She added it to the thirty-four dollars and put it in another sack and wrote "Jacob's Parents" on the outside.

Then Sadie ran back outside and handed the bag to Jacob's parents. "Happy Easter!" she said.

Jacob's family was so thankful. They started crying and hugged Sadie until she thought her ribs would break. Sadie had no way of knowing that Jacob's dad had just lost his job and that this money would help feed them for the week.

Sadie walked over to her mom and cuddled up next to her. "This was the best last Easter egg hunt I ever could have wanted. It's pretty sweet when you can combine fun with helping new friends!"

WHAT DOES THE BIBLE SAY?

Do not forget to do good and to share with others, for with such sacrifices God is pleased.

HEBREWS 13:16

Let's Talk About It

Who couldn't Sadie find at church? _____

_____

What did River say he liked about Easter? _____

_____

Did Cole want to hunt for eggs? _____

What was the new little boy's name? _____

Write down the names of some people you know who help

others. _____

_____

_____

_____

DUCK Commander in ACTION

One of the best ways to show the world the love of God is to do something nice for another person. The Bible tells us that God is love. If we want to be like God, we need to be loving toward others.

One way to show love is to serve others. *Serving* just means helping. When you think of servers, you might think of waiters in a restaurant. That is one kind of server. Their job is to take your order and serve your food to you. But being a server every day is about going out of your way to make someone else feel special. Most people agree that the best way to feel good about yourself is to make someone else feel good. There are many ways you can help others. Look at this list, and choose one you can do today or sometime this week.

★ **Make** cookies for a neighbor.

★ **Write** a thank-you note to your teacher telling her how much you like her class.

★ **Gather** food from your pantry, and have an adult take you to the food bank in your town.

★ **Offer** your mom or dad the night off, and fix supper for your family.

★ **Send** a text to your grandparents telling them you love them.

★ **Draw** and color pictures for the people in your local nursing home. They will proudly display your art.

★ **Do** the dishes after supper—without being asked!

You can think of even more ways to serve others. Remember, God loves a cheerful worker in His kingdom. When you decide to be a server, do it with a smile. Not only will you help others, but you will also help yourself!

CHAPTER 6

The Ski Trip

He has put his angels in charge of you.
They will watch over you wherever you go.

Psalm 91:11 ICB

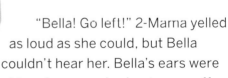

"Bella! Go left!" 2-Mama yelled as loud as she could, but Bella couldn't hear her. Bella's ears were cold, so her mom had put ear muffs on under Bella's hat earlier that day.

2-Mama had no choice but to follow Bella, and that meant going off the ski trail and over a hill to who-knows-where . . .

★ ★ ★ ★ ★

"Please let me be the leader," Bella had begged her mother, Korie, at lunch that day. "I know the way back to the cabin. We've done it for three days now."

Even though Bella was the youngest, she was right. They had skied the same trail over and over for three days. Korie was confident that Bella was ready for the job of leader.

"Okay, Bella," Korie said, smiling at her brave youngest child. "But don't forget that last turn. If you miss it, there's no telling where we'll end up."

And now Bella and 2-Mama were about to find out where who-knows-where was—because Bella had forgotten that last turn.

Korie, who was skiing behind everyone, could see that Bella wasn't going to make the turn, so she yelled to Rebecca, ahead of her, "Rebecca! Don't follow Bella. Go left! Everyone follow Rebecca! Go left!"

Korie said it just in time.

Rebecca and the rest of the kids took the left turn that would take them to their cabin. But Bella and 2-Mama were skiing further away from the group. The only thing Korie could do was wave as 2-Mama followed Bella through the woods and over a small hill. Korie knew Bella would be safe with 2-Mama.

What she didn't know was how they would find their way back to the cabin.

* * * * *

The day had been so much fun. The kids loved skiing with their mom and 2-Mama. Everyone had gotten up early that morning and eaten homemade biscuits and scrambled eggs.

"Skiing takes a lot of energy," 2-Mama said. "Everyone needs to eat a good break-fast so we can make it up and down the mountain."

After breakfast, it was time to put on their ski clothes.

First came the insulated underwear. The boys' long johns, as some people call them, were solid white, while the girls' were pink with tiny blue flowers. No matter the color, all of them were soft and warm and would be perfect for the chilly twenty-four degrees they expected to be skiing in that day.

Next they pulled on their ski socks.

"Only one pair," Korie warned. "Two pairs will make your feet sweat, and then you'll be even colder."

Then everyone wiggled into their ski pants or ski bibs. This important layer would protect them from getting wet when they fell or played in the snow.

But they still weren't totally dressed!

The last step was to put on their coats and hats and gloves.

Korie laughed as she stuffed Bella's long curls into her hat, "It takes a lot of energy to ski, but it also takes a lot of energy to get dressed to ski!"

In their puffy ski coats, the family looked like a room full of colorful snowmen.

"Don't forget your tissues, lip balm, and sunscreen," 2-Mama added. "You never know what the weather will be like on the mountain. It's better to be prepared."

All the kids started stuffing their pockets after 2-Mama's warning. The girls wanted the lip balm that smelled like cherries. The boys searched for the kind that wouldn't make their lips pink. Everyone grabbed tissues and a small tube of sunscreen.

Finally, they were alm-o-o-o-o-st ready.

The only thing left to do was put on their ski boots. Ski boots are heavier than regular boots and aren't very comfortable. No one wants

to wear them longer than they have to, but if you're going skiing, you have to wear them.

"Those are mine," Will said reaching for the bright red boots.

"I know," Bella said. "Mine are purple. I was just moving yours to get to mine."

Getting their boots and skis was a process that happened on the first day of skiing. Everyone's names were put on their skis so no one would get confused. This step is important! Boots and skis have to match up or the skis won't fit properly.

"Let me help you with your socks," 2-Mama said as she smoothed Will's socks and helped him into his boots. "A little wrinkle in your socks could cause a lot of pain." 2-Mama always took the time to smooth the younger grandkids' socks so they wouldn't get

blisters. The older kids had learned that valuable lessons already and checked their own socks carefully.

Now, at last, everyone was ready to ski! The kids and adults grabbed their skis and poles and headed for the door.

"Let's go, kids!" Korie said. "If we don't hurry and get on the mountain, it'll be time for lunch before we even get in one ski run!"

"I'm already ready for hot chocolate," Sadie declared.

"Not yet," her mom replied. "We've got to ski a little first. Remember how we said skiing is more like going to a sports camp than going on a vacation? We've got some work to do before we can get a reward like hot chocolate. So let's go!"

Because ski boots are so heavy, there was a lot of noise as the family clomped their way to the bus waiting to take them to the ski lift.

After the quick bus ride, everyone was finally headed up the hill for the first ski run of the day.

With legs dangling off the ski lift chair, the kids sang Christmas carols loudly as they rode to the top of the mountain. The lift chairs could hold three riders, so 2-Mama rode with John Luke and Sadie, and Korie rode with Will and Bella. Rebecca shared a chair with two people she didn't know who were from Oregon. Everyone was happy that the sun was shining and the air was still. If the wind blows too hard, the chair lift has to shut down and skiers can't get up the mountain.

Soon they found a little hill that was perfect for jumping.

"Watch me!" John Luke yelled as he got up his speed and headed for the jump. "Yahooooo!" John Luke hollered as he flew off the jump.

Korie declared his jump perfect and captured it on her cell phone to show the rest of the family later.

Sadie's jump wasn't so perfect, but she slid down safely in a sitting position. John Luke skied over and tried to bury her in snow as he flipped the snow off his skis onto her head. Korie got a picture of that too.

"John Luke, I'll get you next time!" Sadie squealed as she shook the snow off her head.

At lunchtime the entire family gathered at a restaurant on the mountain. Even the adults and teenagers who had gone skiing on some of the harder runs joined the kids for lunch. Grandpa John, or 2-Papa as the kids call him, Uncle Jep, and Aunt Jessica had skied all morning on the other side of the mountain. They were ready for a break too. The youngest cousins were still in ski lessons, so they wouldn't get to see them at lunch. Everyone would be ready to tell all their ski stories when they were back together at the cabin later that night.

Since the sun was shining, the family decided to eat outside. John Luke got chili for lunch. Will wanted a hamburger. Sadie and Rebecca picked chicken pasta, and Bella wanted pizza. They took their trays out to a table to join the rest of the family.

It was so warm that John Luke took his ski clothes off and sat in the

sun in shorts and a T-shirt. Everyone wore their sunglasses and made sure they had sunscreen on their faces.

"What's been the best part of the day so far?" 2-Papa asked as he gobbled down his fish tacos.

"Covering Sadie in snow," John Luke quickly replied.

"NOT!" Sadie said. "But the jump was pretty cool."

"I like the chair lift," Will told 2-Papa. "And this hamburger."

No one talked much after that. Everyone was enjoying the sun on their faces and the chance to rest their legs.

When lunch was over, Korie said, "Okay, put all your gear back on, guys. You're warm now, but you'll need your coats when you start skiing through the trees. It's not as sunny there."

"Mom, my ears got cold this morning," Bella said. "Do you have an extra hat?"

"I have ear muffs in my coat pocket. Do you want to put them under your hat?" Korie replied.

"Yes, please," Bella said, happy to have the extra layer on her ears.

"It sounds like you kids are giving Mom and 2-Mama plenty of good exercise," 2-Papa said as he popped his skis back onto his boots. "We'll see you back at the cabin this evening!"

And off 2-Papa, Jep, and Jessica went to find some challenging ski runs on the other side of the mountain.

"Let's go find the kids' skiing park," Bella said. "It's always fun. Maybe we'll run into the ski school and we can see Lily and Merritt?"

The kids' area of the park had wooden cutouts of animals for the little skiers to ski around. Will loved skiing around the big bear, and Bella loved the baby deer.

The park also had archways at different heights to ski under. John Luke had to bend down low so he didn't hit his head. The kids didn't find their other cousins, but they had fun anyway.

After everyone had made their way through the park, Korie said, "It's time to head back to the cabin. "Bella is the leader today, so don't get in front of her. And Bella, don't forget that left turn!"

Over the hills and through the trees Bella went. She was doing a good job of leading her family home, but the left turn was coming up, and Korie and 2-Mama could see that Bella was going too fast to make it.

She was having so much fun and skiing so fast, but she couldn't hear 2-Mama warning her of the turn.

And now Bella, with 2-Mama behind her, was headed straight for a hill—and no one knew what was on the other side.

"Bella, slow down! That's a drop-off up there!" 2-Mama yelled, trying to warn Bella, but the warning came too late.

2-Mama saw Bella go up the hill and then she seemed to disappear. 2-Mama skied as quickly as she could to catch up with Bella. She was worried Bella had fallen and hurt herself.

When 2-Mama got to the top of the hill, she looked below to see a frustrated but safe Bella trying to climb back up the hill. "Thank goodness you're not hurt!" The hill was steep, but Bella had skied right over it and then sat down just before she skied right onto a road meant for cars, not skiers.

"Are you okay?" 2-Mama asked.

"I'm good," Bella replied, looking at her surroundings. "I decided to sit down like Sadie did on that jump. I didn't want to end up on the road! It didn't hurt at all, but how am I going to climb back up this hill?"

"Good question," 2-Mama said. "We'll figure it out."

✦ ✦ ✦ ✦ ✦

Korie and the rest of the kids made it back to the cabin safely. By then 2-Papa, Uncle Jep, Aunt Jessica, and the other cousins were all there too.

"Where's Bella?" they all wanted to know. "And 2-Mama?"

"We're not sure," Korie said. "She was leading the way but forgot the last turn. 2-Mama followed her. They're together somewhere, but we're not sure where."

2-Papa checked to see if his cell phone had service. Calling them would be the easiest way to find them. "No signal," he said, holding up his useless phone.

"What can we do?" Korie asked.

2-Papa knew that if Bella and 2-Mama had skied to the right instead of the left, they'd end up on the road.

"Let's go find them," 2-Papa said. "They can't climb their way back to us. They'll have to be on the road somewhere. Who wants to go with me?"

"Me!" All the kids answered as they ran to the car.

★ ★ ★ ★ ★

2-Mama looked around from the top of the hill. She was surprised to discover they were on the road she knew must lead to their ski cabin, but she didn't know exactly how far they were from the cabin or which direction it was.

Next she checked her cell phone. No service, just as she suspected.

There was nothing left to do but carefully ski down to Bella and take off their skis and walk.

"Go ahead and take your skis off," 2-Mama yelled down to Bella. "Wherever we go, we'll have to walk. It's pretty hard to ski back up a mountain."

Once she made her way down the hill, 2-Mama asked Bella, "Do you remember anything about this road?"

Bella looked around, but all the cabins looked the same. And all the bushes and trees were covered in snow. They all looked the same too.

2-Mama didn't want Bella to worry, but she knew it would be dark

soon and they'd need to get inside. Their warm day would soon turn very cold. She decided they needed to start walking toward the nearest cabin. That way they could find a warm place to stay until they could get in touch with their family.

As they tromped through the snow, 2-Mama was proud of how brave Bella was being. Walking in ski boots and carrying skis is hard work, but Bella wasn't complaining at all.

The sun was just about to set as Bella and 2-Mama reached the first house. This made them both happy, but something else made them even happier. Around the corner, they could see a familiar car. It was 2-Papa with a carful of kids!

Bella and 2-Mama started waving their arms like they were workers at the airport trying to guide a plane across the tarmac. They were so happy to see their family and get in the warm car with them.

"Are you okay?"

"How far did you have to walk?"

"What were you going to do?"

"Are you freezing?"

Everyone in the car seemed to have a different question.

That night, around the dinner table, they all had some exciting stories to share about their day of skiing, but Bella had the most exciting story of all. She proudly told her family about sitting so she could safely slide down the hill, walking to find a house for warmth, and finally being found by her family.

"I'm so proud of Bella," Korie said. "Even though she took a wrong turn, she was brave and tried her best, and she followed instructions."

"And, Mom . . . ?" Bella said. "I'm really, really good with someone else leading us home tomorrow."

WHAT DOES THE BIBLE SAY?

Then Jesus told them this parable: "Suppose one of you has a hundred sheep and loses one of them. Doesn't he leave the ninety-nine in the open country and go after the lost sheep until he finds it? And when he finds it, he joyfully puts it on his shoulders and goes home. Then he calls his friends and neighbors together and says, 'Rejoice with me; I have found my lost sheep. I tell you that in the same way there will be more rejoicing in heaven over one sinner who repents than over ninety-nine righteous persons who do not need to repent."

LUKE 15:3–7

Let's Talk About It

Who was leading everyone home on the ski trip?

What did Bella have on her ears that kept her from hearing her mom and grandma yelling to her?

What did Sadie do when she jumped over the hill?

Who went looking for Bella and 2-Mama?

What important thing have you lost? Did you find it?

DUCK Commander in ACTION

Does your mom ever lose her cell phone or her purse? Does your dad misplace his keys or the remote to the TV? When your mom and dad lose those things, they probably ask you to help find the thing that is lost. And when they find what they lost, they're so happy.

Maybe you've lost something important to you like a toy or one shoe or your homework. Everybody loses things, and everybody finds things—even God. It might sound strange to think that God could lose something because He can see everything. He even knows where that lost shoe of yours is hiding!

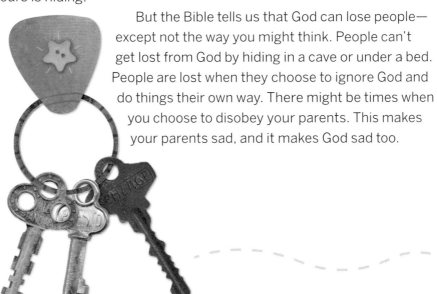

But the Bible tells us that God can lose people—except not the way you might think. People can't get lost from God by hiding in a cave or under a bed. People are lost when they choose to ignore God and do things their own way. There might be times when you choose to disobey your parents. This makes your parents sad, and it makes God sad too.

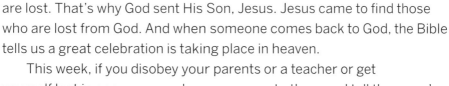

But God never gives up on His children! Just like the man in the Bible who lost one of his sheep but never gave up finding it. God loves everyone! And He is always searching for those who are lost. That's why God sent His Son, Jesus. Jesus came to find those who are lost from God. And when someone comes back to God, the Bible tells us a great celebration is taking place in heaven.

This week, if you disobey your parents or a teacher or get yourself lost in some way, make sure you go to them and tell them you're sorry. It's a way of taking back your wrongdoing and giving it to God. Your parents and God will be so happy!

CHAPTER 7

Lickety-Split

Be completely humble and gentle; be
patient, bearing with one another in love.

Ephesians 4:2

"Mamaw Kay, we're ready!" Bella yelled through the screen door. She didn't normally yell at Mamaw Kay, but Mamaw wasn't on the back porch where the screen door sits. She was in the kitchen, and Papaw Phil was sitting in his big, soft reclining chair watching the weather channel or the news.

The back porch is the first place visitors come when they visit Bella's grandparents. It's a crowded little room that was added on to the house many years before Bella was born. It holds a big freezer that is always full of fish, a water cooler filled with fresh drinking water, an old wicker table for any extra people to sit at during meal time, and at least ten cases of soft drinks for all of Mamaw Kay's guests.

Most people down at the Robertsons' don't stay on the back porch for long. Everyone who comes to Mamaw Kay's house wants to get to the kitchen to taste whatever she's been cooking for the day.

On this day, Mamaw Kay was busy putting a big pan of homemade macaroni and cheese in the oven. The girl cousins love Mamaw Kay's macaroni and cheese almost as much as they love her banana pudding, and since they were spending the night, Mamaw Kay was making both!

"Coming!" Mamaw Kay hollered. "I'm putting the pan in the oven now."

Bella flew off the porch and ran across the yard. "She's almost ready!" This was a big day, and the girls wanted everything just right when Mamaw Kay and Papaw Phil came over.

Bella's grandparents, Mamaw Kay and Papaw Phil, live on the river. Not by the river or close to the river, but right on the river. In fact, during the

rainy season, the river gets so high that it sometimes comes all the way up to the house.

When that happens, the only way out of their house is by boat. But this particular spring, even though it had rained, it hadn't been one of the rainy years. The river stayed exactly where is was supposed to stay, leaving plenty of room for the grandkids to play in the yard around the house.

Mamaw Kay knows the children love to play games, so she keeps the badminton net up and ready for when the cousins come over. She also keeps little jelly jars on the steps of the back porch. They are the perfect size for capturing fireflies or baby lizards in the summertime.

Each cousin's name is written on a jar with a permanent marker. That way no one argues about which jar belongs to which grandkid.

And of course, the kids love to play with the family dog, Bobo. Mamaw Kay treats Bobo like he's one of the grandkids. She likes to talk baby talk to him, and sometimes the girls dress him up like he's a baby and make him ride in the stroller Mamaw Kay keeps in the playroom. Bobo never complains. He's a good dog and is happy to play with the girls.

But of all the places to play at Mamaw's house, the girls now had a place that was their very own.

A few months earlier, Mamaw Kay had come up with a brilliant idea.

"Papaw Phil, let's fix up the little house next door so the girls will have a playhouse. Wouldn't that be fun?"

At first Papaw Phil thought Mamaw Kay was silly. "Miss Kay, that house is so old. Those girls don't want that old house. I don't see how that would be fun." Of course, Papaw Phil's idea of fun is never to play inside a house. He would much rather be outside, in the woods, hunting or fishing.

But when Mamaw Kay asked the girls about it, they jumped and cheered and ran into the living room and smothered Papaw Phil with hugs.

"I didn't know I agreed to this," Papaw Phil said, laughing, with four pairs of arms closing in around his neck.

"I think you just did," Mamaw Kay said, smiling at Papaw Phil and his armload of granddaughters.

"Papaw Phil," Lily said, cuddling up close, "when the playhouse is finished, you can come over and we'll give you a manicure."

Everyone laughed!

"Thanks but no thanks," replied Papaw Phil. "How about I come over and you give me some pecan pie?"

"Yes!" the girls squealed.

"Well, Miss Kay," Papaw Phil said, "you'd better get started. Call Tony. He's a great carpenter and will give you a good price."

Soon the construction was underway. The girls decided they wanted the little house to look like a café. The walls were painted a soft white, and the old floors were cleaned and polished to look brand new.

Mamaw Kay found two round café tables at a garage sale, and the girls declared them perfect. Each table had four chairs with a swirly, curly metal design on the back. A friend of Mamaw Kay's made curtains out of pink fabric with white polka dots. She also made matching cushions for the chairs. One

pink bean bag was set off to the side for anyone who wanted to read. Mamaw Kay loves books and would make sure there were plenty in the café.

But one part of the café was extra special—the Diva Duck Blind. Pink tulle netting separated the Diva Duck Blind from the rest of the café. Behind the tulle netting, the girls put their calculators and cash registers. They decided that Mia and Merritt would be in charge of the cash registers while Bella and Lily would take the orders. And all the girls would help Mamaw Kay make cookies and cupcakes and pecan pie to sell in their café.

The finishing touch was a hand-painted sign to hang over the front door. The sign said "Lickety-Split." That was the name of the new café: Lickety-Split.

The girls wanted the café to have a fun name. They had thought about other names like Boomerang and Willowly-Woo and Jittety-Jig, but everyone agreed Lickety-Split would be perfect.

And it was. The girls were so excited and made plans to spend the night with Mamaw Kay the following weekend. It would be their grand opening.

But then the unexpected happened.

The very night the café was finished, a terrible storm blew through Louisiana. Rain came pouring down and the wind blew until a tree that sat right beside the new café couldn't take it anymore and crashed down on Lickety-Split, crushing one side of the freshly painted, fancily decorated, and soon-to-be fun-filled café.

Mamaw Kay called her son Willie the next morning. "I have bad news for the girls. A tree fell on the café last night. It's not completely ruined, but it'll need some major repairs."

When Willie told the girls later that day, they were very sad. They had been so excited about the upcoming weekend and playing in the café.

"What happens now?" Bella asked.

"Now it has to be rebuilt," Willie said, ruffling Bella's hair. "It'll take probably another month. You girls will just have to be patient."

So the girls waited.

And waited.

And waited some more.

And finally the month passed—quicker than the girls thought it would. They were finally ready for the grand opening!

Bella, Lily, Mia, and Merritt put the finishing touches on the café and anxiously waited for Mamaw Kay and Papaw Phil.

"They're coming!" Bella said. "Hold up the sign!"

The sign read:

THANK YOU! We love our new playhouse, and we LOVE YOU!
Bella, Lily, Mia, Merritt

"Oh goodness!" Mamaw Kay exclaimed. Papaw Phil and Mamaw Kay were so surprised to see their four granddaughters holding the big sign and wearing even bigger smiles.

After lots of hugs, Papaw Phil said, "Well? Where's my pecan pie?"

The girls took Papaw Phil's arm and led him to the table where his pecan pie was waiting.

"And guess what, Papaw Phil?" Mia asked. "You don't even have to pay for your pie."

Papaw Phil laughed as he took a giant bite of pie.

WHAT DOES THE BIBLE SAY?

Be still before the Lord and wait
patiently for him.

PSALM 37:7

Let's Talk About It

Why did the girls have to wait on the new playhouse?

_____

Do you think Papaw Phil wanted to rebuild the house for

the girls? _____

What does Mamaw Kay love to do? _____

What do the kids like to catch in glass jars?_____

What is something that is hard for you to be patient about?

_____

_____

_____

_____

_____

DUCK Commander in ACTION

Being patient very challenging sometimes, isn't it? Having patience means being able to wait for something even though you want it right now. Sometimes when we aren't patient, we might get angry or frustrated and complain. God does not want us to behave that way. He does not like complainers! God wants us to learn to wait patiently and to be happy even when things don't work out like we want them to.

We might ask God for something, but He is smarter than we are and knows it's not best for us to have all the things we want right when we want them. We have to be patient and wait for God to choose the perfect time (or show us a better or different thing He has for us). The good news is that being patient is something everyone can learn! Here are a few tricks you can use to learn how to be patient:

1. Use a timer, either on a watch or in your kitchen. When you think you might have to wait for something, maybe for your mom or dad to come help with your homework, set the timer for five minutes. You may be surprised to realize that five minutes isn't really that long. And you can go do something else while you're waiting!

2. Create waiting a game. When you have to wait, like at the doctor's office or in a restaurant, play a game. I Spy is a good one. In this game, one person spies or sees something and gives clues to the other players until they can figure out what he or she spied. Another good game is the rhyming game. One person picks an object he or she can see, like a tree, and the other people try to rhyme words with that object. For instance, *tree* rhymes with *me*, *see*, *knee*, and *three*. See how long you can keep it going! Before you know it, your waiting will be over.

3. Play board games, not video games. Playing board games like checkers or Chutes and Ladders will teach you how to be more patient. These games require more thinking and quiet time than a video game does.

CHAPTER 8

The New Kid

"Do for other people what
you want them to do for you."
Luke 6:31 ICB

A new kid showed up at school. His name was Fritz, which was funny because it rhymed with grits and in Louisiana, most people like grits. But the new kid didn't get the joke because he had never even heard of such a thing. Even after Bella and the other students described the food to Fritz, he still looked confused.

Fritz looked confused a lot on his first day in their fifth-grade class. Who could blame him?

It was October, and the short kid with big curly hair had just moved to Louisiana from the state of New York. The kids in Bella's class thought he had an accent. He thought they were the ones with the accent. And it wasn't just his accent that made him sound different from the other kids. He never seemed to finish his sentences. Plus, he didn't look at the kids when they spoke to him. And he cleaned his ear with his finger!

"That's weird," one of Bella's friends whispered.

"He's so strange," another one said.

Bella tried to talk to him before lunch, asking a question that might get him to say something.

"Did you bring your lunch?"

He gave her a look as if he was smelling something bad, then shook his head. "I never pack a lunch. I'm allergic to—."

Fritz mumbled something Bella didn't understand. Was it peanuts or wheat or pea soup or Wheaties? The boy then turned and walked away from her as if he didn't want to talk with her in the first place! Bella shrugged her shoulders and went to find her friends.

At lunch, some of the boys in Bella's class were making fun of the way Fritz was dressed. She hadn't noticed it before, but he was wearing the sort of shoes you'd wear to church, the kind of loafers 2-Papa, her grandpa, might wear. His black pants were a bit too short on him too. She told the guys to stop it, but they didn't listen.

In class that afternoon, when the teacher asked Fritz about where he had come from, he gave a not-so-nice answer.

"It's a lot better than West Monroe," he said without looking at any of the kids sitting around him.

"Why do you feel that way?" the teacher asked.

Fritz just shrugged, and his face grew red. He didn't seem to have an answer. "Because, uh, people just—they know more things where I'm from."

Several kids in the class broke out into laughter. The teacher decided to change the subject and move on.

When Bella got home that afternoon, she told her family about the new kid.

"He's so weird," she said as they all sat in the kitchen together.

"Be nice," Korie told her.

"But he is! He thinks he's better than everybody. He didn't want to talk to anyone. I tried . . . but he just walked away."

"Maybe he's just shy," Bella's mom said.

Bella shared what Fritz had said about West Monroe, and then later, when he had told a student his school had learned all about factors of numbers last year.

"He acts like he's smarter than the rest of the kids!" Bella said.

"You know what they say, right?" Korie said with a smile. "Don't judge a book—"

"—by its cover." Bella joined her mother in finishing the sentence. "I know. But it's not

just the cover I'm talking about."

"Sometimes the way we act covers up how we're feeling deep inside," Korie said. "Fritz is probably just nervous about attending a new school and missing his friends and old home. This was just his first day. Put yourself in his shoes"

Bella immediately thought about Fritz's funny shoes.

Later that night, right before bed, Willie came into the family room where they were all watching TV. Bella ran and gave him a hug. He had been gone for a few days on a business trip. Willie immediately started telling the family about this trip. He started laughing out loud as he told them about a man he met on the plane ride home.

"I sat next to a businessman on the plane today," Willie said with a big grin. "He was a young guy in an expensive suit and some pretty fancy shoes. The moment he sat down next to me, I could tell what he was thinking. *Who is this guy with the beard?*"

Everyone laughed. It wasn't the first time they'd heard a story like this.

Willie continued. "I knew he didn't recognize me. He's probably never heard of the Robertsons or Duck Commander. He was literally leaning the other way in his seat, like I had some kind of skin disease. I know I put on deodorant this morning, so I guess my long hair and beard made him think he was sitting next to a weirdo."

The whole family laughed again.

"At first, I was going to mess with him and see if I could get him talking, but I was so tired from all my meetings that I decided to be quiet. The flight attendant came by and recognized me and started talking to me. Suddenly the businessman seemed very interested."

Willie continued to tell them the rest of the story. The young man

introduced himself, and they had a great conversation. It turned out he worked for a company that had opened a new branch in West Monroe. Willie gave him some tips and suggestions and also told him to come by Duck Commander sometime. He'd give the guy a tour.

"The last thing the guy in the fancy suit said was that he had been a bit scared about sitting next to me," Willie said with another chuckle.

Bella looked at Korie and noticed her looking back and smiling. Bella didn't have to wonder what her mom was thinking.

The next day at school, Bella waited with her friends to see when Fritz got to school. She had talked with them and told them the story her dad had shared about the guy on the plane. She reminded them

that they didn't really know the new kid, so they needed to give him a chance. Some of the kids in their class probably wouldn't try, but they needed to be examples and do the right thing.

When they saw Fritz walking down the hallway, Bella and her friends walked up and greeted him with an enthusiastic "Good morning! How ya doin'?"

The poor kid looked terrified.

Maybe it was a bit too much. But they were trying!

Bit by bit, throughout the day, Bella tried to be friendly to Fritz. She asked him about his family and where he was from and what his parents did. It turned out his parents had recently divorced. Fritz was the oldest of four children, and they had moved with their mother to Louisiana. Bella could tell the boy seemed sad about everything, but

also he sounded like he was trying to be strong for his mom and his younger brothers and sisters.

The rest of the class, even the boys who had been making fun of him the day before, seemed to understand things a bit more when they heard about Fritz's family. He still managed to say some crazy things in class, like how his dog supposedly weighed as much as a bull or how he loves Saltine crackers dipped in pickle juice. He also still did that weird thing with cleaning his ears. But Bella knew it was important to give him a chance to fit in.

Fritz would find his place in their class. Bella would help make sure of it.

WHAT DOES THE BIBLE SAY?

But the LORD said to Samuel, "Do not consider his appearance or his height, for I have rejected him. The LORD does not look at the things people look at. People look at the outward appearance, but the LORD looks at the heart."

1 SAMUEL 16:7

Let's Talk About It

How would you feel if you had to move and change schools in the middle of the year? _____

How did Bella try to get to know Fritz on his first day of school? _____

What happened to Willie on the plane ride? _____

_____

Can you think of someone you barely know who might be different than you think? _____

What could you do to try to get to know that person?

_____

_____

DUCK Commander in ACTION

Maybe you've heard the saying "Don't judge a book by its cover." That just means that the outside of the book might not look so interesting or might even look kind of strange or uninviting, but the inside might be amazing! Some of the greatest books of all time have simple titles and ordinary covers. But when you take the time to read them, they turn out to be incredible and inspiring stories, the kind you don't want to end, the kind you continue to think about long after you finish.

People can be this way too. Nobody should be judged by the way they look or sound or behave. It takes time and real communication to know what a person is thinking and feeling. Ask questions and listen to answers. Be patient and caring. Not everybody will be your best friend, but that doesn't mean you can't try be a friend to everyone.

God could easily judge all of us because He sees everything about us—and not just the good stuff, but the bad stuff as well. He sees our cranky sides, our mean spirits, our jealousy and pride. But God overlooks this because of His Son, Jesus Christ. God never judges a book by its cover because He already knows the pages of our story. He loves us and forgives us for all the mistakes we make, those in the past and those we'll make in the future.

If the maker of the heaven and earth and everything else can look past our covers, we can certainly do the same for the people we come in contact with each day. You never know what you'll discover when you stop making assumptions and start trying to get to know someone. Look

around this week for someone you could get to know in a closer way. Maybe there's someone in your Sunday school class or neighborhood that you haven't taken the time to get to know. Don't be afraid. Go right up to them, and ask how their day is going. You might be surprised by how the conversation goes. And you never know . . . that person could be your new best friend!

CHAPTER 9

Music Lessons

Listen to advice and accept correction.
Then in the end you will be wise.

Proverbs 19:20 ICB

All the instruments sat at the side of the music room, waiting for the kids in music class. Instruments from violins and violas to flutes and clarinets to saxophones and bells and drums lined the tables and chairs.

I want to play the bass drum! ten-year-old Willie thought, eyeing the large round percussion instrument that was always his favorite to watch in the marching band.

Today the fifth graders had come to the music room to try out some instruments. This was the first year they could be a part of the elementary band, so they were here to learn about all the varieties of musical gear in front of them.

When the music teacher told the kids to select an instrument, Willie stood up, ready to run to the instrument he wanted.

Oh no!

"Line up alphabetically," the teacher announced casually, as if it wasn't a big deal. But it was! Willie's last name started with an *R*, all the way at the back of the line!

Of course . . . Willie thought. *Why do we always have to do things alphabetically?*

By the time Willie got to the musical instruments, all that was left was an oboe with way too many buttons to push, a French horn that looked far too complicated, and a tambourine.

Come on, Willie thought. *Everybody knows how to play a tambourine!*

Only one other instrument was left—a massive tuba that looked as big as him. And that's what he chose.

As the kids got settled, the music teacher went through all the instruments, explaining how to play them.

"When it's your turn," he said, "do your best to play your instrument. And don't worry how it sounds. It's everyone's first day!"

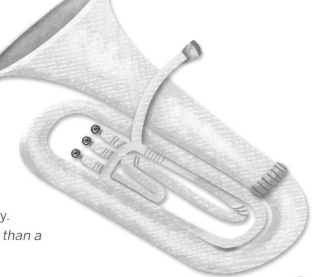

Willie was really nervous all of a sudden. He had never played any sort of instrument before, especially one he had to blow in. But he'd give it a try.

It can't be much harder than a duck call, he thought.

When Willie's turn came, he picked up the tuba. It wasn't as heavy as he thought it would be—but it was just so BIG. He placed it on his lap with the wide opening facing the music teacher.

"You're not firing a gun, Willie," the teacher said as the kids around him laughed. "You don't want to bend your body to reach the mouthpiece. Bring the tuba to you."

With the teacher's help, Willie got the instrument in the right position. Then he took a deep breath, opened his mouth, and blew into the wide mouthpiece.

The only sound that came out was his huffing and puffing, and his face turned bright red. Not a peep was heard from the tuba, however. The kids laughed again.

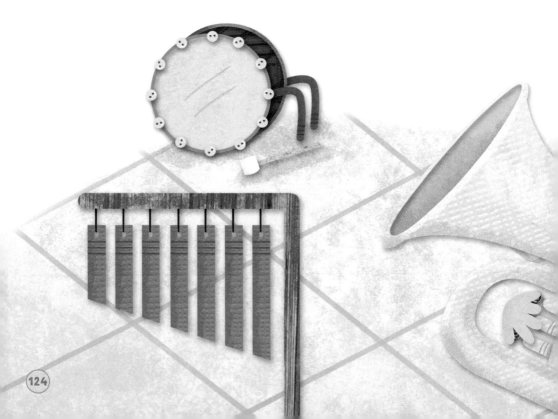

"No, no, no," the music teacher said. "You have to close your lips. Don't open your mouth like you're eating a hamburger. And don't let your cheeks puff out."

The teacher cleaned the mouthpiece and put it up to his mouth to show Willie exactly how it was done. He made it look so easy.

"Remember, close your lips and keep blowing and vibrating your lips until it begins to play," the teacher explained.

Willie tried again. And again. And again. Soon his head was spinning, and he couldn't get any more air out of his lungs. But the tuba remained silent. Not a squeak of anything sounding like music came out.

"Let's move on," the music teacher said. "That might not be the instrument for you, Willie Robertson." He moved on to the next student.

But Willie was determined! Later that day, he managed to get the tuba to make a sound. But it sounded kind of like a dinosaur burping after a big dinner. Or maybe a siren with a fading battery blaring . . . and then trailing off. Each note Willie honked out would suddenly begin to go badly. Very badly.

It didn't matter. Willie wasn't giving up!

The teacher let Willie take the tuba home, where he practiced even more. He was quite a sight, carrying the tuba home on the school bus.

Willie's mom, Miss Kay, tried to be patient, but finally she encouraged him to find another instrument.

Anything else.

A harp.

A xylophone.

A keytar (that's a keyboard and guitar combined).

But Willie wasn't interested. He wanted to learn the tuba. One afternoon, Phil heard him playing in his room. He opened the door to Willie's room as if there was a fire blazing under the door.

"It sounds like someone's dying in here!" Phil said.

"I'm trying to learn to play, Dad," Willie gasped, barely making a sound. He was out of breath from practicing so long.

"Son, I believe with God's help, you can accomplish anything. But God also gives us common sense, and that sense should be telling you that playing the tuba just isn't in the cards for you."

"I'm not giving up," Willie said.

"Well, okay then," Phil said. "You can practice as long as you want—in the woods."

So day after day, during music class and in the woods, Willie practiced. His fingers fumbled with the keys, and he couldn't get his breathing right. The sound the tuba made never got smoother or prettier. It continued to sound like a howling dog. He finally got tired of the endless advice his music teacher kept giving him. Over and over the teacher kept saying for him to play "legato." Apparently legato was the opposite of what Willie was doing. *Legato* means playing the instrument in a smooth and flowing manner.

Legato. Legato. Legato.

One day, Willie realized that the word *legato* sounds a lot like a saying he had heard: "Let it go . . ."

Maybe it was time to let it go. So Willie decided to tell his music teacher that he wanted to stop playing the tuba. His music teacher believed in finishing what you start, so Willie was ready for a speech about not giving up and dreaming big dreams and working hard.

But Willie's teacher simply smiled and said, "I think that's a good decision, Willie. A really good decision."

Dreams and drive and goals are all good things. But at an early age, Willie learned an important life lesson. Sometimes you simply have to let some things go— especially things that sound like a big dinosaur burp.

WHAT DOES THE BIBLE SAY?

For the LORD gives wisdom;
from his mouth come knowledge
and understanding.

PROVERBS 2:6

Let's Talk About It

For a moment, picture Willie Robertson playing the tuba.

Okay . . . picturing it? We got that out of the way!

What's one dream or goal you have that seems impossible?

_____

Have you ever tried to do something and it hasn't worked

out? What happened? _____

_____

Who does God say we should put our trust in? _____

_____

What are some ways you can determine if something you

want to do is a good idea? _____

_____

_____

DUCK Commander in ACTION

Nobody wants to be considered a quitter, especially because we're encouraged to never give up and to aspire for greatness. We see sports figures holding up trophies and talking about the desire to win. We watch people trying out for competitions and blowing the judges away, whether it's singing or dancing or doing a trick.

Everybody is told to follow his or her dreams.

The truth is that Phil's advice to Willie is good life advice for everyone: God gives us a mind to understand our own limitations and realities. Someone might dream of being a star basketball player,

but his or her short size and lack of speed—and complete inability to ever make a basket—should tell him or her otherwise.

Here's another thing God wants: He wants the best for us. And that means doing what is commanded in Proverbs 3:5–6: "Trust in the LORD with all your heart and lean not on your own understanding; in all your ways submit to him, and he will make your paths straight."

This verse makes one thing very clear: we're not to lean on our own understanding or what we *want* to be true. Instead, we're to realize that God knows what's best for us. This is true whether you're a kid or an adult. Sometimes the things we want, no matter how noble or right they might seem, aren't the things God has planned for us.

Make of list of the things you'd like to do while you're a kid. Maybe it includes playing a sport or learning how to ride a horse or becoming a painter—whatever you'd like to do. Next, talk to your parents about making those dreams become a reality. Pray about it and ask God to open and close doors when necessary. Then, when God does open or close a door, be grateful for His guidance.

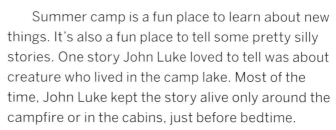

CHAPTER 10

The Prank

*Teach me knowledge and good judgment,
for I trust your commands.*

Psalm 119:66

Summer camp is a fun place to learn about new things. It's also a fun place to tell some pretty silly stories. One story John Luke loved to tell was about creature who lived in the camp lake. Most of the time, John Luke kept the story alive only around the campfire or in the cabins, just before bedtime.

One year, however, John Luke decided to bring the creature to life. He thought it would be great to have some fun with the campers. So he went for it . . . without giving it much thought.

It's always best to think through a plan before you go through with it. John Luke would soon learn why . . .

★ ★ ★ ★ ★

The night before the prank was to take place, John Luke started to tell the story at the campfire about the creature from the lake. It was a dark night, and the black woods surrounded the campers. The only sound they could hear was the crackling of the fire and an occasional owl *whoot-whooing* in the trees. John Luke waited until all the campers were quiet and then began the tale of the dreaded and monstrous alli-beaver.

"The beast has haunted these very woods for a hundred years, occasionally coming out of them to scare campers," John Luke said, shadows from the campfire flickering across his face. "He is half alligator and half beaver and has thick hair and sharp teeth and eyes that look like the coals in this fire."

John Luke lowered his voice and used his most dramatic storytelling skills. "And the alli-beaver can swim very fast."

A few campers giggled nervously as he talked about the alli-beaver, but he ignored them as he gave the history of the forest creature. For fifteen minutes, John Luke told of the mysterious animal who lives in the woods but loves to swim.

"The camp directors won't tell you about this creature," John Luke continued. "But it exists. There really is an alli-beaver, and he can be anywhere. He might peek in your cabin window late at night, or

he might glide through the water while you're boating or fishing. He's everywhere. And sometimes . . . he's very, very . . . HUNGRY!"

Everybody jumped when he shouted the word *hungry*. And then everyone laughed because John Luke's face looked so funny as he tried to scare them.

The stage was now set. Tomorrow John Luke would go through with his grand plan.

★ ★ ★ ★ ★

John Luke had found a wolf costume at the costume shop earlier that year. It was used, so it wasn't very expensive. Yes, it did smell pretty yucky, sort of like the way your socks might smell after a hot day of playing outside. The costume also required that John Luke have a friend to help him put it on and zip up the back. But it also allowed for some tweaks . . . that would make the alli-beaver come to life.

And another thing: the wolf costume was heavy. Really heavy.

Right after lunch, John Luke got one of the camp counselors to help him get into the outfit. He knew there'd be free time and some of the kids would be boating in the lake down the hill. He planned on sneaking down there before anybody arrived, getting in the water, and hiding behind the dock at the edge of the shore. Once someone got in the small boat and drifted out to the middle of the lake, the alli-beaver would strike!

Thanks to the thick fur on his costume, the water didn't feel as cold as normal as John Luke slowly slipped into the lake. He carefully walked into the lake until the water was up to his shoulders. Then he waded over to the edge of the wooden dock, grabbed on to the ledge, and waited. Sure enough, several campers showed up.

This is going to be perfect! John Luke thought.

It was especially perfect since the two campers getting in the boat were Jenny and Pam. Earlier in the week, Jenny and Pam had sent John Luke a box at mail call with a bag of Skittles—only the Skittles had been replaced with raisins and John Luke hated raisins. It was payback time for John Luke's friends.

The girls took their time rowing the small boat out to the center of the lake. The deepest point in the lake was around forty feet. When John Luke saw Jenny and Pam facing the other way, he began swimming toward them.

About midway between the dock and the boat, John Luke began to

sink. His head bobbed under the surface of the water, and he paddled to resurface. John Luke was a good swimmer, but his skills were no match for the heavy costume.

When costume got wet, it also got heavy—very, *very* heavy. This problem should have been obvious—if only John Luke had thought the whole thing through!

John Luke struggled to keep above the water, and soon he was safely back on the shore. He started ripping off the hairy mess and noticed the two girls laughing at him.

"What are you doing, John Luke?" Jenny yelled from the middle of the lake.

"Were you trying to scare us?" Pam asked.

John Luke joined them in laughing. He was going to say something, but he just coughed instead. He took a deep breath and thanked God that his fun idea hadn't ended up drowning him.

That wasn't the last time John Luke wore the hairy costume, but it was the last time he would go swimming in it. In fact, it was the last time he would ever go swimming in any kind of costume. From then on, all costumes stayed on dry land.

John Luke realized that some ideas—as creative or silly or clever as they might seem—aren't the best ideas. Some ideas are just plain bad. That's why you have to think before going through with something. If he had, John Luke would have realized the obvious.

An alli-beaver might be able to do a lot of things, but he can't swim.

And a true alli-beaver would be smart enough to know it.

WHAT DOES THE BIBLE SAY?

The way of fools seems right to them,
but the wise listen to advice.

PROVERBS 12:15

Let's Talk About It

Are alli-beavers real? (**Of** course not, unless you're in West Monroe, Louisiana.) _____

Was John Luke's idea a good one or not? Why?

_____

What's the last "big idea" you had? What happened?

_____

Can you think of a time when you decided to do something and realized later it wasn't a very good choice?

_____

What should we do before we make a decision?

_____

_____

DUCK Commander in ACTION

All of us like to have fun. If you come from a big family like the Robertson family, you're probably used to brothers and sisters and cousins playing pranks on each other. Most of the time, the pranks are harmless and hilarious. But occasionally a prank can be a very bad idea. It can be dangerous, like John Luke's prank turned out to be, or maybe even mean-spirited.

Not one thing is wrong with an idea when it first pops up in your head. You might suddenly think, *I want to do that!* in the middle of class or on the way home or during your summer camp session. It might be a high place you want to jump off or a firework you really want to light or a friend you want to prank. It could be a hundred thousand different things.

1. **The key with any idea is to not act upon it right away.** Think it through and figure out whether it's actually a good idea. If a friend asks you to go do something and it seems crazy or dangerous, you need to stop and think about it first.

2. **God wants us to make the right decisions.** He wants us to be smart. This means asking those who are older and wiser what they think about our ideas. Surprises are fun, but sometimes they can be disappointing or even dangerous. Parents, grandparents, and even older brothers and sisters are there to give advice. So are teachers and neighbors.

3. **The next time you get some grand plan in your head (like putting on a costume and scaring campers in a boat), think it through carefully.** Ask others for their thoughts. Pray about it too—even if it seems silly. God hears every prayer and shows us answers, whether it's through wise people around us, through the Bible, or through basic common sense.

CHAPTER 11

Leap of Faith

When I am afraid, I put my trust you.

Psalm 56:3

Sadie looked out onto the bridge with a terror she had never felt before. Her feet were planted firmly, and she was determined to not move them.

"There's no way I'm walking across that," she told her family.

It was the fifth day of their summer family vacation. It's no family secret that Sadie is afraid of heights, anything that moves faster than she does, and the ocean. Today's journey across a bridge was exciting to John Luke, but to Sadie it seemed like her family had lost their minds.

The horseshoe-shaped bridge wasn't very long. In fact, it would take only about five minutes to walk across it. But five minutes seemed like an impossible task to Sadie.

"You can do this!" Willie said, halfway telling himself the same thing. He wasn't the bravest in the family either. In fact, when Willie was a teenager, roller-coasters scared him. But he knew Sadie would be fine.

The bridge was ten feet wide and had walls on each side that were over five feet tall. Sadie could barely see over the wall. She looked down the center of the bridge and could see lots of tourists enjoying the view and taking pictures. Everyone was laughing and talking.

Why it this so hard for me? Sadie asked herself.

The reason was obvious. The platform—the part of the bridge you walked on—was made of glass. See-through glass. That meant Sadie could see all the way down—to the ground. The five-foot-high walls were no help when you're four thousand feet from the ground. That's like being on top of your house times about two hundred!

"Can the glass break?" John Luke asked their Hualapai Indian guide. It was a fair question and one Sadie was interested in knowing the answer to. After all, they had driven several hours to get to this place in Arizona. They needed to know how safe it was.

"Absolutely not," their guide said. "This bridge can withstand an 8.0-magnitude earthquake! The walkway can carry over 800 people, but we allow only 120 people at any given point." He looked at the group with a smile. "And this super-strong glass was hand-crafted in Germany."

The tribal guide was very confident telling the family about the Grand Canyon Skywalk. His tribe, the Hualapai Tribe, owned the bridge, so he knew what he was talking about.

But none of that mattered to Sadie.

The guide could have told Sadie that angels had come down and built the bridge themselves. There was no way she was stepping onto an invisible walkway thousands of feet above the ground below.

One by one, Sadie's family members slid on the slippers they had been given to protect the bridge and stepped onto the invisible walkway. Soon, Sadie and Korie were the only ones still waiting at the opening edge, a strong wind whipping their hair.

"Just don't look down," Korie told Sadie.

"But I still have to look out!" Sadie said. "It freaks me out just standing here looking out across the canyon."

The other side of the Grand Canyon was miles away. The walkway didn't go to the other side; it was too far away. The walkway just made a loop out over the canyon. The majesty of God's creation was breathtaking. So was the height where they stood.

"Nobody is going to force you to go," Korie said. "But you know God will protect you. Plus—it'll be something you'll always remember!"

Korie started to walk very slowly onto the thick glass. Sadie could hear Bella squealing and watched as Will and John Luke jumped up and down. *Boys!* she thought. She was having a hard time breathing, much less thinking of jumping up and down!

The guide could see how nervous she was. He stepped up beside her to provide some comfort.

"What's your name?" he asked.

"Sadie."

"Sadie, my name is Levi-Levi. Let me ask you a question. What are you most afraid of in life?"

Sadie breathed in and continued to look out at her family appearing to fly over the Grand Canyon. "Right now, that bridge!" Sadie said without hesitation.

"Do you know that the best way to conquer our fears? To attack them head-on!"

Wow! Sadie thought. *He sounds like 2-Mama.*

Sadie's grandmother had once shared a very helpful quote with her when she was afraid to try a back dive: *Do the thing you fear, and the death of fear is certain.*

Do all older people know this about fear? she wondered.

The guide continued, "In this case, conquering your fear means you need to tackle your fear of heights. One way to do that is to look at the truth surrounding the thing you fear. This walkway can't move. The glass won't break. It's safer than the bus you took to get here. So your fear isn't of the bridge itself but of the drop below it. Right?"

Sadie nodded.

"I know you can do this," Levi-Levi said. "Every day, we have to believe in something and then take a chance. We have to step out into the unknown. So, Sadie—will you take my hand and take a leap of faith with me?"

Her body continuing to shake and her legs heavy with worry, Sadie took the older man's strong grip and began to walk with him. He reminded her time and time again, every few steps, not to look down, to remember that the bridge would not fall, and to stare out at the beauty of the land surrounding her.

Sadie continued to hear her mother's encouraging words as well: "God will protect you."

She slowly began to walk faster and feel better. Something about the guide's reassuring tone calmed her. The glass beneath them didn't move a bit, even as the wind continued to blast all around them. She could hear her family's applause as she and Levi-Levi got closer to the other side of the walkway. Sadie didn't turn back; she just kept walking, holding the hand of the kind guide.

When they reached the end, Sadie breathed a huge sigh of relief as her parents and siblings surrounded her.

"See? You can now say you walked across the skywalk!" Levi-Levi said.

She gave the man a hug and thanked him. "I can't believe I did that."

Levi-Levi returned her hug. "You had to believe that the bridge wouldn't fall in order to take that first step. With each step, you believed you could walk across. Everything about what you just did required faith."

Before leaving the skywalk, Sadie had to do something. She slipped the slippers back on her feet and took just a few steps out—by herself, just enough to be able to see the incredible drop below. This time she looked down, staring through the clear glass toward the bottom of the canyon. Then she looked back out at the remarkable view.

God created all of this! she thought. *If He can do something that amazing, He can definitely watch over me and protect me.* Sadie just had to remember to always trust and believe Him.

Sadie didn't spend much time on the glass though. She had taken a leap of faith already. Now she wanted to come back down to earth and maybe see the Grand Canyon from below. One time walking across this skywalk was enough for her! But she did it—and she would never forget.

WHAT DOES THE BIBLE SAY?

"Lord, if it's you," Peter replied, "tell me to come to you on the water." "Come," he said. Then Peter got down out of the boat, walked on the water and came toward Jesus. But when he saw the wind, he was afraid and, beginning to sink, cried out, "Lord, save me!" Immediately Jesus reached out his hand and caught him. "You of little faith," he said, "why did you doubt?"

MATTHEW 14:28–31

Let's Talk About It

What's the tallest thing you've ever stood on? What about the biggest thing you've ever seen? _____

_____

When was the last time you were really afraid of something? _____

Is it difficult to trust in God when you're afraid?

_____

Is anything coming up that might make you nervous? What is it? _____

What's the best thing you can do for those nerves?

_____

DUCK Commander in ACTION

Remember a time when you were afraid of the dark?

Maybe the darkness still makes you a little scared at bedtime. What sort of things does your mother or father say to you to help you not worry? Maybe:

"There's no reason to be afraid of the dark."

"Nothing's going to happen to you."

"We can leave this light on and the door open."

"I'm right here if you need me."

That last statement is perhaps the best thing to remember—not just about a fear of the dark but for any fears period. God wants us to know He is always there. And the truth is the He knows we need Him. He just wants us to remember that ourselves.

Do you have a big test coming up? Or a big game you're nervous about? Did the tire on your bike just go flat and you have no way of buying a new one?

Or maybe it's bigger stuff. Your parents might be getting a divorce. Or maybe you're getting ready to move to another school or another state.

The next time something comes up that makes you afraid, take Levi-Levi's advice. Think about all the facts about the event (maybe even write them down!). Knowing the facts—the truth—will help you be less fearful. Then remember Philippians 4:14: "For I can do everything through Christ, who gives me strength."

There is nothing we can't do if we trust in Christ.

CHAPTER 12

Open and Honest

Truthful lips endure forever, but a lying
tongue lasts only a moment.

Proverbs 12:19

Willie Robertson was having one of those days at work. His morning meeting had gone twice as long as he had planned. Then he had to spend thirty minutes on the phone with one of their top customers concerning a lost shipment of Duck Picker Duck Calls. *How could two thousand duck calls suddenly go missing?* he asked himself. Did a commando force of ducks swoop in and snatch them?

Now that Willie had finally had time to work on some of the tasks in his office, his cell phone suddenly rang.

It was Korie. "You need to pick Bella up from school."

"Why? Is she okay?" Willie asked with concern.

"She has an upset stomach and feels like she's going to throw up."

Willie shook his head. "Oh, come on. She's not sick."

"She was complaining about going to school last night," Korie said.

"Bella's fine," Willie continued.

"Well . . ." Korie said. "She's waiting in the school office right now."

Willie looked at all the phone calls he had to make and the stack of papers he needed to go through. He didn't even want to look at the hundreds of e-mails waiting for him.

"I can't leave work now, Korie."

"Well, I definitely can't pick her up," Korie said. "Neither can Mom or Dad."

Korie and her parents were in New York on a business trip. The other kids were in school. Willie began to go through the list of people who might be able to pick up their daughter, but everybody was either busy or gone.

"You can leave the office for a few minutes," Korie said. "She sounded really sick."

Willie knew he needed to do the right thing and pick her up from school, but he still had his doubts.

And the moment he saw Bella, Willie knew.

She's not sick. Not even a tiny bit.

The nine-year-old wore a smile and looked as healthy as any fourth-grader.

"What's wrong?" he asked, scratching his head.

"Let's go!" Bella said as she zipped past him.

Willie barely had time to say hello and good-bye to the ladies in the school office. He wanted to ask them about Bella but then thought again. *They probably know she isn't sick too.*

In the car driving home, Willie looked over at Bella, who sat in silence, staring ahead.

"You okay? Mom said you had an upset stomach. Do you feel like throwing up?"

Bella shrugged.

Willie knew right away that something was wrong, but it had nothing to do with the stomach flu. "Okay, what happened at school?"

She remained silent, staring out the car window.

"Bella, listen," Willie said. "I managed to get out of school a few times myself. I know you're not sick. Something's wrong. Just tell me."

Bella seemed to be thinking about what to tell her father, yet she still didn't say a word.

"You can talk to me," Willie said. "You can always talk to me."

That's when Bella began to cry. *Oh dear,* Willie thought. *Dealing with crying isn't my strongest gift.*

Bella covered her face with her hands.

"Hey—it's okay." Willie took one of her hands and held it while he steered the car with his other hand. "Whatever it is, it's going to be okay."

"It's just . . . I wanted to leave. I don't want to go to school anymore."

"You don't want to go school? Like ever again?" Willie asked.

"Yes!" she sobbed. "I never ever want to go back."

"So you want me to homeschool you or something?" Willie said.

"Yes. You can be my teacher."

Willie couldn't help himself—he howled with laughter.

"That's maybe the worst idea you have ever had, young lady!"

Bella still had tears running down her face, but she glanced over at her father and couldn't help giggling.

"So what's the issue? Are there problems with some of the other girls?"

"I don't want to talk about it," Bella said.

Part of Willie wanted to get upset and tell Bella about how he didn't want to leave work, about how busy he was and how he couldn't afford to be doing this, especially since she really wasn't sick. He wanted to tell her she was in trouble for making up a story to get out of school. But he didn't. He remained quiet. He could tell his youngest daughter was pretty upset. Plus, by the third daughter, he had learned how to be patient and wait for them to talk.

When they arrived home, Bella went inside the house first. She slumped into the sofa and started crying again. Willie stood there to see if she wanted to talk.

I know Dad wants me to talk to him. And he does always make me feel better afterward.

So she decided to tell him the truth—even though she was still crying. "They just ignore me! They act like I'm not even there, and they've been doing this since the start of the year, and I just don't want to go school anymore. I don't want to go back!" she wailed.

Willie sat down on the couch and put his arm around Bella. She cried into his shoulder, and he just let her get it out. Soon Bella began

talking, telling him the details about a couple of her close friends who weren't talking to her and were spending time with only one another and never including her.

"It's going to be okay," Willie said.

"But how do you know that?" Bella asked between sniffles.

"Because I'm going to get those two girls kicked out of school."

Bella jolted upright. "Dad! You can't do that."

Willie smiled. "Okay But, listen. Don't worry about them. If they don't want to include you in things, then choose to be around others who do. If they don't want to be friends with the coolest person in fourth grade, then they have really bad taste."

"No, they don't," Bella said, looking down at her hands.

"Are you defending them?"

"No . . ."

"Bella—we don't want you to lie about what's going on at school. Your mother and I want you to always tell us the truth. Okay?"

"Can you not tell Mom about this?" Bella asked.

"I have to tell Mom," Willie said. "You know that."

"But you didn't tell Mom when you bumped into her car with yours!" Bella said.

Willie nodded. "Yeah, but eventually she found out, and I got in big trouble. Remember? Just like you will."

"You didn't get in trouble."

"I did. I had to go to the repair shop instead of going hunting,"

Willie said. "That was rough."

"Am I in trouble?" Bella asked.

"Only if you stop letting us know what's going on. Okay?"

Bella hugged her father. Then she asked him another question: "Can we go have lunch at the Duck Diner today?"

Bella suddenly looked healthy and happy and ready to tackle anything life might bring. Willie could only shake his head.

"That sounds pretty good," he said. "But since you're 'sick,' it's chicken noodle soup for you, young lady."

WHAT DOES THE BIBLE SAY?

The LORD detests lying lips, but he delights in people who are trustworthy.

PROVERBS 12:22

Let's Talk About It

Was it right for the girls to leave Bella out?

_____

Was it right for Bella to say she was sick when really she

was frustrated at how she was being treated?

_____

Is it hard to talk about some things that are going on in

your life? _____

_____

What do you do when someone catches you lying?

_____

_____

_____

DUCK Commander in ACTION

It's easy to bend the truth just a little every now and then, isn't it? Not to outright lie but to change the truth just a little, maybe leave out a few details. Every day, we're faced with choices that test us. And we can choose whether or not to speak the truth.

Here are the facts: the truth is the truth. Changing the truth a tiny bit doesn't make it a tiny lie. A lie is still a lie—no matter what the size. Our parents and siblings and teachers and friends all want and expect us to always be honest. Ultimately, God commands us to be truthful in everything. And although we might be able to fool other people, we can't fool God.

People lie for many reasons. Sometimes a lie can seem like the easiest way out of a situation. Or a lie might make us look better in some way. Other times we might choose to lie for what we think is a good reason, such as Bella feeling hurt by her friends. She didn't go to school that day planning to lie to her teacher or her parents. Yet as the events of the day happened, she did.

It's also important to talk to those adults who love you and want the best for you. God wants us to talk to Him as well. Pray for strength and help and for anything and everything that might be going on in your life. There's nothing too small for Him to hear or for you to ask Him.

If you have been dishonest about something, now is the time to tell the truth. You'll feel better just talking to someone about it.

CHAPTER 13

New Food

For [God] satisfies the thirsty and fills the
hungry with good things.

Psalm 107:9

When Rowdy joined the Robertson family,
he wasn't very adventurous with food. At
twelve years old, he knew what he liked and
didn't like, and he didn't want to be talked into
eating something new. And there was one food
he didn't want to touch or smell or even see!
He definitely didn't want to taste it.

"Just try it," Sadie said one day as they sat
down for dinner.

Rowdy held his nose and shook his head.
"No way. I hate broccoli."

"I used to hate it too," Korie said as she
dished the vegetable onto her plate. "But then
I actually tried it, and I liked it. And it's really
good for you."

"I'm not a fan," John Luke said, before
adding, "but I do eat it."

Everyone knew John Luke would eat
anything, so he wasn't really much help.

Rowdy thought broccoli looked like a green
alien with curlers in her hair. The thick stalks

sometimes looked stringy and reminded him of what it would be like to eat a small tree. One time, one of his aunts had overcooked the broccoli and it looked like a soggy green mess in a bowl.

Yuck. I'm never eating it! he thought.

Then there was the smell. Rowdy had smelled better smells in a barn. The smell reminded him of the inside of the family Suburban when they had stopped for fast food and left the leftovers in the car overnight. Day-old pickles and mustard and French fries don't make a great smell in the Louisiana heat.

Gross.

Moving in with a new family had given Rowdy plenty of new experiences, and most of them had been great. He was learning how to live with lots of brothers and sisters and cousins, he had gone to summer camp, and he had even flown in an airplane for the first time.

On this particular night, it seemed the entire family had decided it was time to convince Rowdy to try a bite of broccoli.

What is wrong with these people? Rowdy thought. *Why won't they leave me and my taste buds alone?*

"Come on. It's not as bad as you think," Sadie said.

"I'm eating it!" Bella chimed in as she dipped her broccoli in some cheese dip to cover the actual taste of the broccoli.

"I'll give you five dollars," Willie told him, thinking that money always works.

"Will you give me five dollars for eating mine?" John Luke asked.

"No way!" Willie said.

But Rowdy remained strong and determined. All the logical arguments and bribes were not going to work.

"I will never eat broccoli!" he promised. "I know I'll hate it."

"You don't know until you actually try it," Korie said, once again trying to be logical.

Rowdy had never tried broccoli. That was her main point.

A few days later, Rowdy decided to be logical too. He went to

the computer to look for other people who shared his anti-broccoli perspective. He soon discovered a quote from a very famous person.

I can't wait to share this with my parents!

"Do you know who hates broccoli?" Rowdy asked Willie and Korie.

"You?" Willie asked.

"Yes. But no. President George Bush."

Willie smiled. "The father or the son?"

"Uh, I'm not sure . . ." Rowdy said.

"It's President George H. W. Bush," Korie said. "The father of George W. Bush"

"Well, whatever," Rowdy said. "If a president can hate broccoli, then so can I!"

"George Bush Sr. also served in World War II, graduated from Yale University, became a millionaire by the age of forty, then served in many positions before becoming the vice president and then president," Koric said. "If you've done all those things, I guess you can probably refuse to eat broccoli. You, on the other hand, are still a kid, and you need to start eating your veggies."

"Maybe Rowdy's going to be president one day," Willie said.

Rowdy looked down at his shoes. "I'd rather be a millionaire by the time I'm forty instead. And I'm not ever going to eat broccoli!"

Korie smiled. "I bet one day you're going to say you like it," she said, with that tone mothers get when they can see the future.

"Never!" Rowdy said.

Later that night, at the dinner table, Rowdy decided to share more of the findings from his research.

"Do you all know why I hate broccoli?" Rowdy asked.

"Rowdy, we're eating chili," John Luke said.

Sadie giggled.

"I know. But still—I discovered I have a gene that makes broccoli taste bad."

"What?" Bella asked. "That's crazy."

"I didn't know you went to the hospital to get yourself checked out," Willie joked.

Rowdy pulled out the piece of paper where he'd scribbled down some of the details.

"Broccoli and Brussels sprouts—which I hate too—have this thing called *gluck-sign-on-lates* in them," Rowdy read. "It makes broccoli taste bitter to people with this gene called TAS and a lot of numbers. That's what I have."

"First of all, don't say *hate*. That's a strong word for not liking a certain food, and second, what was that big word you tried to say?" Korie asked.

"Yeah. Let me see that," John Luke said, grabbing the sheet and laughing. "It's not *gluck-sign-on-lates*. You pronounce it *glue-so-sin-olates*."

"How do you know that?" Sadie asked John Luke.

"Can I just state the obvious here?" Willie eventually said, as they were discussing how the word might sound. "Rowdy, how do you know

you have this gene if you've never put broccoli in your mouth? You have no idea what it tastes like or if it's bitter to you."

Rowdy shook his head. "But some people have a bad reaction to it! That's gotta be me," he said confidently.

Which gave Willie an idea . . .

★ ★ ★ ★ ★

The following Saturday afternoon, a group of kids came over for some of Willie's homemade pizza. While the pizza baked, Willie served appetizers, including "cheese" dip and chips.

Taking a break from playing a video game, Rowdy ran into the kitchen for a glass of fresh lemonade. Then he glanced at the dip and asked what it was.

"Cheese dip. Dad made it," Sadie said.

Rowdy quickly dipped a tortilla chip into the dip and ate it. He nodded. "Yummmm." And then went back to his game.

Rowdy came back several times for more of that delicious dip.

Later that week, Willie cooked dinner, this time with an awesome new recipe for a ham and cheese biscuit. Rowdy had no trouble eating two or three of them.

The next night, it was a macaroni dish with hamburger and cheese.

"What's up with the new recipes?" Rowdy asked his dad as he

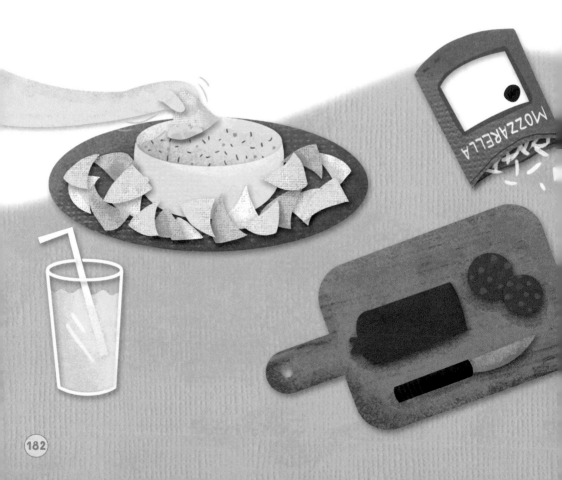

devoured his second plate of the cheeseburger macaroni.

"I thought it was time for all of us to try some new things," his dad answered.

Rowdy took another bite. "As long as it's not you-know-what, I'm good!"

Willie's week of cooking new recipes ended with a special chicken dish. Rowdy was the first person to sit down, expecting another incredible dinner. His dad was a great cook, and these last few meals had been amazing. The whole family prayed and then started passing the food.

"What's this?" Bella asked.

"It's called Chicken Divan," Willie said.

"And what's in it?" Sadie asked.

Rowdy didn't see the smile on his sister's face. Sadie had been in on the trick the entire week and couldn't wait to see Rowdy's reaction.

"I'm glad you asked," Willie said in a rather loud voice. "Well, there's chicken, of course. Mushroom soup. Mayo. Sour cream. Cheddar cheese. Let's see—there's butter. Bread crumbs. Parmesan. Curry. There's even lemon juice."

"It's good," Rowdy said. "I like it." The whole family smiled, remembering how he didn't like chicken when he first joined the family.

"Oh, and one other thing. There's chopped broccoli."

Rowdy stopped chewing even though his mouth was full.

"Whahhhh?" he garbled through a mouthful of food.

Everybody laughed.

"Yep," Willie said. "It has a pound of chopped-up broccoli in it."

Rowdy knew better than to spit it out. Korie would not like that. So he swallowed the large bite in his mouth.

"Wait. I don't taste broccoli," Rowdy said.

"How would you know if you can taste broccoli?" Korie asked. Remember, you've never tried it."

Rowdy looked down at the chicken on his plate and moved it around with his fork. "Is there really broccoli in this?"

"Yes!" everybody at the table screamed out.

"The chicken probably overpowers the taste," Rowdy said.

"No, I think you surprised yourself and you actually do like broccoli, Rowdy," Korie said.

"What? Of course I don't!"

Korie looked at Willie, letting him deliver some additional surprises.

"Remember that great new cheese dip I made the other day?" Willie asked. "Guess what it had inside it?"

Rowdy shook his head.

"Broccoli," Bella said.

"And the ham biscuits?" Willie asked.

Again, Rowdy remained silent, his face in total disbelief. This time Little Will said it.

"Broccoli!"

"And remember the cheeseburger macaroni?" Willie asked.

"Okay, I get it, guys." Rowdy said. "Broccoli?"

"Yep!" Willie answered.

Rowdy thought of his dad's secret plan to make him eat the green enemy he'd vowed never to consume.

Finally he started laughing and realized he had to admit defeat.

"Okay, okay!" Rowdy said. "I guess I actually do like broccoli—if it's cut up really tiny and mixed with other things."

He took another bite of the chicken, then said, "But I'm serious about this. I'm never trying Brussels sprouts. Never."

WHAT DOES THE BIBLE SAY?

Every good and perfect gift is from above,
coming down from the Father of the heavenly
lights, who does not change like shifting shadows.

JAMES 1:17

Let's Talk About It

Name some foods you hate (or think you hate if you've never tried them). _____

_____

What would it take to convince you to try a new food?

_____

Have you ever thought you were going to hate some-thing—until it happened and you discovered it actually was a great thing? _____

_____

Why is it bad to say never? _____

If you haven't already, promise your parents that you'll try broccoli—and some other act of trust and obedience.

_____

DUCK Commander in ACTION

Have you read the Bible verse that tells children to eat their fruits and vegetables? You haven't? Of course you haven't. It's not in there! So why do parents want kids to eat healthy things?

The most obvious answer is because it's healthy to eat nourishing foods. God gave us our bodies, and we're supposed to take care of them. We're supposed to form good habits and not give in to the temptation of too many nachos or sugary treats.

This story isn't just about eating the right food though. It's also about not being stubborn and being willing to try new things. You'll have many opportunities in life when you could refuse to do something that is actually good for you to do. Eating a vegetable is a simple example. But sometimes we can be stubborn about bigger issues and remain stuck in one place, afraid of what the outcome might be if we just try.

bonjour!

God's people, the Israelites, were like this. The Bible tells us time and time again that God would tell them to do something and to obey Him, but they would refuse to listen. They'd go their own way. They wouldn't trust in God's plans and promises. Because of this, the Israelites had to learn the hard way and pay the price for not obeying.

1. **Listen to your parents and teachers when they urge you to do something—whether it's trying something out for the first time or doing a task in a different way.** Catch yourself if you're being close-minded or stubborn, and make a different choice. Life is all about figuring out what God wants for our lives.

2. **Look for something new to try this week.** It might be a different food or singing a new song or learning to say hello in another language. Or it might be stepping out and being helpful and obedient in a way you haven't tried before.

3. **Never say never!** Because you just might try something for the first time and discover you love it.

CHAPTER 14

Little

Don't let anyone look down on you because you are young, but set an example.

1 Timothy 4:12

The big brothers could do everything. But Jep Robertson couldn't do a thing.

His oldest brother, Alan, already had his driver's license! But the only thing five-year-old Jep could drive were his Matchbox cars.

Jase, who was thirteen, was in seventh grade and had been able to see *Star Wars* and *Raiders of the Lost Ark* in the theaters the weekend they were released. Jep could only watch reruns of *Bugs Bunny* and *Looney Tunes* cartoons on television.

Willie, who was eleven, was playing basketball on his

school team. Jep could barely dribble a regular basketball, much less make it into the actual hoop.

Jep didn't like being the youngest brother. It meant he was the smallest and the slowest and the last when it came to everything.

"You're more spoiled than the three of us combined!" Alan once joked.

Jep refused to believe it.

"Momma doesn't want you to get hurt," Jase told Jep one day after he got angry about being left out of the brothers' backyard football game. "We all know she loves you the most."

Jep didn't like to hear his brothers tease like this.

"Enjoy being young, Jep," the ever-wise Willie told him. "Getting old can be tough."

Jep was confused by Willie's comment.

"You're only eleven!" Jep said.

"Yes. And trust me— that's old! I'm in fifth grade. That's when you know a lot."

Jep wanted to know a lot too.

One Saturday, when his brothers had gone into the woods and left Jep behind, Phil noticed

Jep playing by himself.

"That is the saddest face I have ever seen on any child," Phil told him. "What terrible thing happened?"

"Nothing . . ." Jep said.

"Surely something happened," Phil said. "Did your bike blow up? Or did your mother decide to set all your toys on fire? Or did a black bear kidnap your brothers and leave you behind?"

Jep tried to conceal his smile. "No. But I wish a bear had done that. The boys leave me out of everything 'cause I'm little."

Phil spoke to his youngest son for a few minutes to try to cheer him up, but nothing would do. Finally, he had an idea.

"Get your shoes on, Jep."

"Where're we going?"

"We're going hunting," Phil said.

This was exciting since Jep had never been hunting before. His older brothers had, but Jep was still waiting to be old enough to actually put on camouflage and have a gun and wait for the ducks. Phil drove the two of them out to a swamp, but Jep soon realized they weren't going duck hunting.

"What are we doing?" Jep asked Phil.

"I told you. We're going hunting."

Phil gave Jep some tall rubber boots to put on. He wore the same.

Jep knew they weren't going duck hunting because Phil didn't have all his gear with him. No rifle and no painted face. Not even a duck call.

"What are we hunting?" Jep asked.

Phil gave him a fishing net. "You'll see."

They took a boat out deep into the swamp. Soon Phil stopped the boat and pointed to a small tree loaded with fruit that resembled small, dark red crabapples.

"What are those?" Jep asked as they got closer.

"Those are mayhaws."

Phil pulled a few off the tree and gave them to Jep. They were half an inch long.

"Why are they called mayhaws?" Jep asked.

"What month is it again?"

"It's May."

"That's right," Phil said. "That's when they ripen."

"Can I eat it?" Jep asked.

"Sure. Go ahead. But they don't taste good raw. We'll make the best jelly out of these berries though."

Jep had eaten the jelly before, but he'd never thought about how they got the jelly.

"So we're hunting for mayhaws?" Jep asked.

"Yep. And I'll show you how we do it!"

Phil stood up in the boat and carefully balanced himself. Then he grabbed one of the bushes and shook it. Dozens of the red mayhaws dropped into the water and floated on the surface. Phil did this several times until they were surrounded by the berries. Then he handed Jep the fishing net.

"Okay, Jep. Start hunting."

Jep began to scoop the tiny fruit out of the water, dumping them into a bucket. Soon the bucket was overflowing.

"What do we do with the berries?" Jep asked Phil.

"You'll see."

It would be the following day before Jep realized the true fruit of his labor. The family all sat together for their Sunday dinner, where

Miss Kay had prepared everything from chicken and dumplings to her famous homemade biscuits. And they now had something special to put on those biscuits: mayhaw jelly.

Everybody loved it.

"This jelly was hand-picked by the best mayhaw picker in the land," Phil said. "Jep Robertson."

The four jars of jelly were devoured. The boys all wanted more, but Miss Kay told them they needed to pick more mayhaws if they wanted more jelly. So they decided they'd go that afternoon.

As they were cleaning up dishes, Phil pulled Jep aside from the rest of the family.

"Did you like the jelly?" Phil asked him.

"Oh, I loved it," five-year-old Jep said.

"And where did that jelly come from?"

"The mayhaws."

"That's right," Phil said, raising his hand and showing Jep the red mayhaw in his hand. "That very thing you love so much came from this tiny, little thing. Isn't that amazing?"

"Yeah, it is," Jep said.

"So just remember something. Being small can be a blessed thing. God has a purpose for every single thing He's created, big and small. Just because you're small—even as small as this little

mayhaw—doesn't mean you can't be used in a very big way."

Jep stood there, his eyes wide open, gazing at the red berry.

"So next time your brothers give you a hard time or leave you out of something, you just think of this mayhaw, okay?" Phil said.

"Okay."

"And tell them if they keep it up, we're not going to share any jelly next time!"

WHAT DOES THE BIBLE SAY?

"It is like a mustard seed, which is the smallest of all seeds on earth. Yet when planted, it grows and becomes the largest of all garden plants, with such big branches that the birds can perch in its shade."

MARK 4:31–32

Let's Talk About It

Do you ever feel too young or too small? How does it make you feel? _____

Do you have older brothers or sisters? How do they make you feel? _____

Can you think of other things like the mayhaw berries that are small but can turn into something big and special?

_____

Why should you never feel like you're too small?

_____

What is something great about your age? _____

_____

_____

DUCK Commander in ACTION

Have you ever felt too small or too young to do something? Have you ever wished you could just grow up and know more and be better at things?

All of us have felt that way! Even adults sometimes wish they were stronger or better at different things in life, maybe a sport or a hobby or their job.

Like Phil told Jep, God has a purpose for everything He has created. Every one of us is made in God's image, and we are meant to celebrate that. We are meant to honor and worship Him. This includes being happy, happy, happy with who we are right this very instant.

Jesus told the parable of the mustard seed to show his disciples that they were part of God's family and kingdom. They were small—so very small that things looked scary—yet they were helping the kingdom to grow. Each disciple had a very special place in God's kingdom, and each one had been chosen to do his part in helping to make Jesus known to the world.

You may be small, but you can fit in places where others can't. You may be young, but you have the energy and excitement that older people might not have. You may be weak, but God still gives you strength in everything you do.

We live in a world that encourages us to be faster and stronger and brighter. But don't ever forget about the mayhaws, the tiny fruit just waiting to be picked from a tree and used for something special.

As a Christian who trusts Jesus, you can be used in a very mighty way with other believers to share the story of Jesus with others. Never forget that Jesus was once young and small too. He knows exactly what it feels like. Yet He asks us to trust and rely on Him every day.

Never forget what the young David said to the mighty warrior Goliath when he stepped out to battle him: "You come against me with sword and spear and javelin, but I come against you in the name of the Lord Almighty, the God of the armies of Israel, whom you have defied" (1 Samuel 17:45).

You are never, ever small or insignificant when God is on your side.

This next activity will take a few months, but it will be fun! Trace your hand on the paper. You might need an adult to help you. Put the paper in a special place, and take it out one time every month for a year. Keep drawing your hand on top of the hand you already drew. It will be fun to see how much you grow in a year!

A Final Note

We hope you've laughed a lot as you've read these stories about our family. And we hope you've been reminded of some of your favorite stories about your own family! More than anything, our prayer is that you've learned more about God's love for you and His will for your life.

Here's the best part: God gives you a blank piece of paper where you can write your life story. Isn't that cool? And you get to start new every day! In fact, why don't you start right now?

Pay attention to how God is working in your life. You will be amazed at His goodness, His grace, and His creativity. Life is like a roller-coaster ride sometimes, but if you keep God at the center of your life, you will be able handle any ups and downs. Thank you for letting us play a small part in your life story by telling you how God has worked in our lives.

If you have other questions about God, please talk to your parents, a youth minister, or your pastor. They will be happy to help you.

Hugs and Blessings,
Korie and Chrys

Dear God, You are our hope for a better tomorrow and our comfort for any troubles today. We need You and ask that You guide our steps, guard our hearts, and protect us. In Jesus' name, Amen.

★ ★ ★ MY STORY ★ ★ ★

★ ★ ★ MY STORY ★ ★ ★

★ ★ ★ MY STORY ★ ★ ★